# *Ganado Red*

# Ganado Red

A Novella and Stories

Susan Lowell

Foreword by Phillip Lopate

*Designed and Illustrated*
*by R.W. Scholes*

MILKWEED EDITIONS

GANADO RED


Printed in the United States of America.
Published in 1988 by MILKWEED EDITIONS.
Post Office Box 3226
Minneapolis, Minnesota 55403
*Books may be ordered from the above address*
91 90 89 88 5 4 3 2
ISBN 0-915943-26-3
Library of Congress Catalog Card Number: 87-63531

Publication of this book, the first Milkweed National Fiction Prize winner, is made possible by grant support from the Dayton Hudson Foundation for Dayton's and Target Stores, and by support from the Jerome Foundation, the Arts Development Fund of United Arts, and by the First Bank System Small Arts Funding Program.

The author wishes to acknowledge the publication of several of the stories in this collection in the following publications:

"The Castle of the Fairy Queen," *Tucson Weekly*, January 7, 1987; "The Kill," *Montana Review 8*, Fall 1986; "Lavinia Peace," *Arizona Quarterly*, Autumn 1987; "Los Mojados," *Writers' Forum*, Fall 1986; "La Tejedora," *Arizona Quarterly*, Summer 1986.

To R., A., and M.

## FOREWORD

"Eureka!" one is tempted to shout when, called upon to judge a pile of short story books—for the most part creditable but mundane—one suddenly comes across a manuscript that is so clearly better, truer, more vibrant than the rest. What made me fall in love with Susan Lowell's stories almost from the start? Partly it was the tension in her prose, alert with original images and justly chosen words, her sentences rearing and coiling back instead of lying minimally flat. Partly it was the mature confidence, the plenitude and warmth of her narrative voice. But mostly it was the mounting danger I felt when sucked into each of her tales, that peculiar throat-swelling sense of "What's going to happen next? How can she possibly resolve this quandary?" which is the mark of the storyteller's art, just as the sensation of the top of one's head spinning off is the proof of the poet's.

Each of these stories is alive with danger. The suspenseful construction of Lowell's narratives keeps raising the ante, taking us where we want to but fear to go—even when, as in her "Lavinia Peace," the situation is no more violent on the surface than two estranged sisters going through some old family mementos. Paradoxically, we are made to share the profound isolation of each character, while brought to understand potentially nourishing, potentially destructive links with a wider community, a web of history and kinship. In the world of these stories, all relationship carries with it a Jamesian threat to the fragilely achieved, breakable self—especially as domination, calculation and indifference are always on the horizon—but at the same time, release from self-entrapment constitutes the old wild hope.

Sometimes the threat *is* the love relationship: the sudden fraying of trust between man and woman. In "A Circle, a Square, a Moon, a Tree," for instance, we watch the harsh competitiveness of two graduate students, both writing dissertations, who just happen to be lovers living together. Sometimes the threat comes from illness, bodily betrayals. In "White Canyon," the only first-person story in the book, the narrator moves between childhood and adult wounds, trying to find an explanation for her brain tumor. Even after her skull has been trepanned and put together, one senses there will always be a crack in perception—a missing puzzle piece. Sometimes the threat is larger, ecological, like the radiation fallout in "White Canyon" or the condo desert developers in "Wild Pigs." Whatever the starting-point, we are brought face to face with the realization, as one character keeps repeating in "Marble," that "Things are very fragile."

For all this exploration of vulnerability, Lowell's fictional art seems to have grown far beyond the "walking wounded" to encompass a much more solid, noble and grounded vision of human possibility. In her two best stories to date, "Los Mojados" and the title novella, "Ganado Red," she demonstrates an astonishing range and sympathy for very different lives. All the main protagonists, sociologically speaking, of the Southwest—the American Indians, the Mexicans, the old white ranchers, the hippies, the neo-liberal capitalists—are represented in the form of complex characters. "Ganado Red" is particularly brilliant as it modulates from a certain Gothic mood of darkness and menace (especially in the uncanny, Poe-like section, "The Castle of the Fairy Queen") toward the resignation and humorous continuity of the everyday. This historical novella tells us volumes about the commodification of a craft object, as it follows one Navajo rug from its impoverished woman weaver, through its first principal owners, two wealthy "old maids" in the D.H. Lawrence/Taos set of the 1920s, on to a fascinatingly cold Santa Fe dealer, and finally coming to rest in the dazed, middle-class arms of contemporary yuppies.

I should say something solemn here about the author's feeling for the land, but since I am a thorough urbanite who feels more comfortable with subways than wildflowers, and who usually falls asleep when reading what I am tempted to call the "narcissism of landscape," I will only add that Susan Lowell's place descriptions do not put me to sleep. On the contrary, she has a sharp, passionate way of dramatizing countryside and its fate. Though she ranges from Utah to Princeton to Texas, it is finally the area around New Mexico and Arizona which seems to root her fiction most. I kept thinking of a later-day Willa Cather, both in her complex human portrayals and her attachment to that landscape. Another writer Susan Lowell brings to mind is Alice Munro, because of her tough, unsentimental humanism—her insistence on recording both cruelty and connection—and because of the satisfactions of craft which the true short story writer brings to that much-abused form

—Phillip Lopate

# *GANADO RED*

*Eight Stories*

# White Canyon

I

Two dead deer were hanging in the juniper tree outside the window. They had appeared in the night.

Screaming, my little brother and I escaped from our cribs, built toe-to-toe by our father at the front of the trailer, and we crashed into our parents' bed in the back. We lived on the rim of White Canyon, in Utah, almost a day's drive from the nearest town. As recreation from hunting for uranium, some of the other geologists in the camp had gone hunting for deer and had hung the carcasses in the tree. Our parents explained that the deer would be made into jerky, which we ate often, powdered like us with fallout from the nuclear tests going on in Nevada, farther west.

One deer dangled upside down, roped by its miniature hoofs. The other was suspended apparently in mid-leap across a branch. Their legs were dry sticks, their fur iron.

Fifty yards from the trailer camp, the ground fell away suddenly, but I do not remember the canyon as white. The cliffs were streaked and layered: rust, pink, bone. The Little Colorado River glistened like a knife at the bottom. My brother and I were forbidden to go to the edge of the canyon alone.

In St. George, Utah, two hundred miles southwest of us, parents roused their children from bed to watch the atomic explosions bubble up in the sky. It was as good as the Fourth of July.

We never saw a mushroom cloud. Sometimes violent rainstorms swelled the Little Colorado, washed out the road to town, and turned the camp into sticky red mud that glued my brother's boots in place until he was rescued.

In a small deckle-edged photograph we play beside the trailer, and our big spaniel watches us. I hold my arms akimbo; a straight black ponytail sprouts from either side of my head. My brother, wearing a knitted cap, sits behind the wheel of a bulldozer built from an orange crate.

When my father nailed on the finishing touch, an empty Vienna sausage can for a smokestack, my mother cried: "It's perfect!"

And although the snapshot shows them as gray, I know that my denim jacket was marvelously studded with jewels of red plastic. In the picture I am three; my brother is eighteen months old.

Memories, like snapshots, are always in the present tense.

I stare upward through bars, and several strange adults stare down. Something is happening. I am a prisoner, a freak, a specimen. Where is my mother?

At St. Mary's hospital in my parents' home town of Tucson my brother has just been born.

The can of evaporated milk is too heavy for my hand. It slides into the bassinet on top of him and causes a surprising amount of noise.

The three of us fly north again to meet my father, who works for the Atomic Energy Commission. The airplane is silver, like our trailer, but narrower and somewhat longer. The stewardess wears a heavy navy blue uniform and a round wool cap. I glare suspiciously as she dares to hold our baby.

Those trailers were just that, not pseudo-houses. Besides beds, ours contained a tiny galley and a bathroom. A table unfolded beside a sofa, where the dog slept, and every spare inch of wall was fitted with small cupboards of irregular sizes, in blond wood with stiff latches. We owned few possessions and each had its place. At night my doll and my brother's truck disappeared into a cupboard beyond our reach.

For weeks I checked the juniper tree as soon as I woke in the morning. One up, one down, the deer hung in my nightmares.

My father's Geiger counter sometimes served as a doorstop. It was the size of a shoebox, with wrinkled black paper skin and glass-covered dials marked in arcs of red numbers against a sallow green background. It was too heavy for me to lift.

The narrow aluminum door opened high above the ground. Even to reach the step my brother and I must stretch our legs. A dozen other trailers surrounded ours, housing couples and families; across the Colorado Plateau in the early Fifties the uranium boom was on, and it had generated jobs for young engineers, physicists, and geologists. Exploring for mineral deposits was a much better job than working underground, my father thought, and he began to dream of graduate school.

The catskinners — Caterpillar tractor operators — lived together in a barracks near the mess hall and wash house. Some of them were Navajo Indians; their reservation lay south of us. But we were not near anything.

My brother and I traveled in the back seat of the Jeep with the dog, who would start each long trip on the floor, gradually moving up to the seat and pushing my brother to the floor and me to the corner. Then our mother would restore us to the original order, and the process would begin again. When we hit bumps I clung to the rim of the seat with both hands. I could feel the shape of a pipe beneath the thin padding.

On a map of the Four Corners area I know these names: the Bear's Ears, the Valley of the Gods, Moab, Shiprock, Gallup, Lukachukai, Chinle.

Outside the window the mesas seemed to be carried past upon a tray. Clouds formed another landscape. Bound by barely visible wires, power pole giants marched in single file. There were two kinds: male and female? But which was which? They reminded me of the pair of Hopi kachinas that my parents kept in one of the highest cupboards at home.

My brother and I made up a song for riding through dips: "Uppee go—downee go!" Because of the way our father drove, we had to sing it fast. Our stomachs flipped pleasurably.

We were always driving straight for a pool of shining water across the pavement ahead of us. It always faded before the splash, which I never stopped expecting.

Real water was brown. I knew that. And I knew that before we forded it my father would stop and wade impatiently across it to make sure that the Jeep could pass.

Once, when we moved to White Canyon, we towed the trailer onto a ferry and crossed a wide river. My mother preferred to stay in the car with the baby, but my father and I rode outside.

In my memory, the wind lifts my bangs from my forehead. The ferry is made of rickety wooden latticework. The water looks like torrents of chocolate whipped into little waves and blobs of creamy foam, but it smells like mud. I enjoy looking at it; I have no fear of falling in.

Once a month we used to drive to the small town of Blanding to shop. Because of the size of the trailer refrigerator, we only ate fresh food one week in four, and my brother and I drank diluted canned milk. It still tastes of childhood to me. Much of our fruit was dried, and the big glass jar of jerky was kept low enough for me to reach for snacks.

The road from Blanding to White Canyon turned into dirt and then got rough. A tall sign stood at this point, and when my uncle came out from medical school in Boston to visit us, my mother took his picture there.

It is summer. He wears a white T-shirt, and the old color transparency film has put blue highlights in his black hair. Deadpan, he lolls against the signpost, while above his head the text jumps out of the brilliant sky:

DANGER AREA
Four-wheel-drive vehicles mandatory.
Before entering, leave notice of your whereabouts.
Carry food and water.
Blinding sandstorms and flash flooding may occur.
Do not attempt to cross dips when flooded.
Proceed at your own risk.

The sign told us nothing new. I did not understand why the adults found this scene so remarkably funny, both then and each time the slide snapped into focus on the screen afterward. Now I see. In Boston the picture was a trophy. My uncle's foot was planted casually upon a beast. And to my parents, too, it stood for adventure, a push at the limits, the joy of laughing at dangers survived, or discovered to be imaginary after all. And youth: they were twenty-six; he was twenty-four. Neither failure nor grief had touched them closely yet.

The shadow of the Jeep used to stretch across the buttes, with our necks and heads pulled into long grotesque shapes. Then it would tumble onto flat ground—a fleeing box with two large and two small loose pegs inside. At the sight or sound of us, deer like giant jackrabbits went lofting through the scrubby trees. Coyotes melted away. Vultures sliced their invisible circles overhead.

"Buzzards in the sky know the time is nigh," my mother used to sing.

My uncle's summer visit coincided with a plague of stinging gnats so bloodthirsty that they kept us briefly indoors. The adults sat and talked. I played with my doll, an eight-inch blonde with a snarled wig.

My uncle pointed at the Geiger counter.

"But what about the hazards in this job?" he asked.

"Hazards?" said my father.

"Radiation exposure. You're dealing with uranium, aren't you?"

"Small amounts," said my father, shrugging.

The A.E.C. had given his team a fleet of Jeeps and plenty of money, and he enjoyed the field work, climbing up and down the canyons and deducing the patterns in the rocks. Once he found an Indian pot no bigger than a walnut tucked in a niche in a cliff. Inside was a pinch of dust, perhaps the remains of a sacrifice long ago.

At night my brother and I used to swarm into his khaki lap and tug out the hand lens he always wore on a chain around his neck. The steel cover glided off a disk of magnifying glass about the size of the ball of his thumb, where swirls of whitish ridges ran beside pink ditches where I could almost see the rush of blood. The sofa cover was as coarse as a basket. My mother's wedding ring was uninteresting. But two kinds of freckles spotted her arm, uniform round dark ones and pale ones with irregular edges like stains.

My hands strongly resembled my father's, even down to the network of lines in the palms. Longer, more slender, my brother's hands had crooked little fingers hereditary in my mother's family.

Sometimes we looked at the grains that, crushed together, made rocks. I learned that yellow meant uranium; red, iron; blue, copper. Then the rocks would return to the pile of canvas sample sacks in the corner where the pick also leaned. Recently another pick had shattered against a rock and lodged a splinter of steel in my father's chin, which bled when he shaved.

My little brother ran away one day. Turning from the clothesline, our mother saw only me. The search and panic spread through the camp to the edge of White Canyon. Finally someone found him playing pinball in the mess hall with a Navajo catskinner who had caught him on the path to the cliff.

The first fallout storm came at about that time. In a camp full of Geiger counters it was impossible to miss. Suddenly one morning they all began to chatter: radioactive particles showered us, three hundred miles downwind from the nuclear explosions over Nevada.

Hiroshima and Nagasaki had been bombed eight years before, and the implications of fallout were clear enough to people with scientific training, though not perhaps the implications of low dosages. In a way it was still an innocent age. There was a residue of awe—and of V-J Day. Also, familiarity breeds carelessness. Everyone in camp knew about the Nevada tests. Yet the Atomic Energy Commission was everyone's boss; the object of the job was to find uranium, the source of the problem. They had never agreed to be contaminated, but there seemed to be no escape. Perturbed, everyone stayed indoors until the radiation level dropped off, like the gnats, and life returned to normal.

There were many picnics, one in the middle of a skeleton of the carnivorous dinosaur Allosaurus. It lay on its side like a chicken with a three-foot skull, and suddenly after lunch all the young geologists started a rock fight with fossils.

I think that my mother, who had majored in anthropology, suggested our trips to a Hopi snake dance and to the Gallup Ceremonial. My clearest memory is of a Navajo squaw dance.

I ride on my father's shoulders above the heads of the crowd. The other men all wear black cowboy hats with wide flat brims. Some of the women are dressed in velvet blouses; their long tiered skirts sway as they move. I stare at the other children. A bonfire streams into the night sky, a drum beats, and the dancers take a few steps forward and a few steps back. My brother and I lie upon a sleeping bag at the fringes of the orange light. A few steps forward, a few steps back. I pry open my eyelids. Can it be that my parents are dancing too?

Another time, a sing or curing ceremony for a sick young girl was held at her home. This I remember only faintly, having been told the details years later. We arrived at dawn, and there was little to see besides the other visitors and their wagons and pickup trucks. The sand painting and singing had all been done inside the round log hogan. But as the sun came up we did watch a shaman throw the girl's clothes out of the smoke hole at the top of the hogan. They caught a breeze and drifted to the ground, and she was purified.

The second fallout storm was heavier than the first. It was impossible to stay indoors long enough. When my father ran the Geiger counter along the dog's back, the needle surged up the green dial, and the machine clicked faster. My parents looked at each other.

A letter arrived from my uncle.

"Can't you evacuate?" he wrote. "Why don't they warn you before blowing off these bombs?"

"They don't know we're here," my mother suggested.

"It's like getting an X-ray," said my father.

In Washington President Eisenhower observed that it was probably just as well to keep the public in the dark about atomic matters—confused about the difference between fission and fusion, as he put it.

More fallout came down. My father started to apply to graduate schools. He might, he explained, become a rock doctor. I puzzled over this and finally abandoned the mystery as insoluble. Rocks could not be sick or hurt, I was sure.

My doll is shut in the high cupboard, and I am alone in the trailer. I know that I should not climb upon the back of the sofa and from there find a toehold on the cupboard handle. Clinging to the wall with my right hand, I stretch out the other toward the door that hides my doll. My fingers graze her silky hair.

Slowly, slowly, guiltily I lose my balance. I fall. The bone above my left eyebrow strikes the floor first, and a lump swells up. My mother is not angry. My brother peeks past her knee. I have a headache, I am sick, I turn green. Someone mentions the word "Blanding."

"He's out in the field," my mother says.

She means that my father has gone to work.

Another man, a neighbor, is driving us in a strange Jeep. At first my eyes behave oddly; they seem to see through water. Each hill is endless, vertical. Jolt by jolt, my head ringing, we fight against gravity. But as the hours pass I begin to feel better. We arrive in Blanding at dusk and find the doctor. I lie on a silver table, his face balloons in mine, and then a horrifying instrument—a needle?—stabs straight at my eye but misses.

II

"Who's the president of the United States?"

I struggled through layers of murk, broke the surface, and answered: "Jimmy Carter."

Then I gave a start. The baby was in the bed with me! No, she wasn't after all. My arms were empty, but I felt a great pain behind my left eyebrow.

The man sitting across the room from me made no response. I recognized him now; he wore a gold Rolex watch big enough to manacle both my wrists at once. I had met him in the emergency room. He was a neurologist.

"What's the date today?" he asked.

I struggled again. The sky was blue outside. The baby had been born in this hospital at night, but that was weeks ago, before my head began to hurt. I seemed to have paused in the midst of a long journey. Was it one or many nights that I remembered like a blow in the diaphragm?

"I'm not sure. August, 1980."

"Where are we?"

"Dallas, Texas."

I had a house, a husband, and a job teaching poetry. I lived on a street called Hillcrest, which was quite flat. My students, who drank Dr. Pepper for breakfast, included one excellent poet.

"What drugs have you taken?"

"Ice!" I said angrily. "That's all. What's the matter with my head?"

"We're working on that."

He never looked at me directly except when he shone a penlight in my eyes. When he had gone I lay back and listened to the interminable discord inside my head.

I remembered how once in a museum of medical curiosities I'd seen the skull of a Victorian railroad worker who was brained by a crowbar and survived. Also bequeathed to science, the crowbar neatly fitted into the cleft it had made.

Needle marks speckled the inside of my left arm. A large television screen tilted over me. Someone had arranged the cushions of an easy chair in the shape of a bed upon the floor.

A nurse came to collect a flabby ice pack from a pool of water on the table beside me. She was not the tall black woman capped with a purple wig who had brought the ice the night before. No other painkiller was allowed. It might confuse the diagnosis.

"Where's my mother?" I said, beating down panic. "And my husband? And my baby?"

"Did they check you in last night?"

So it had only been one night. Memories jammed against one another without logic, the dial flipping from channel to channel. I must have acted strange yesterday afternoon.

The headache spirals me up a peak impossibly narrow and steep, but I refuse to go to the hospital. Clenching her fists, the baby screams and sweats.

I am holding a telephone. My doctor uncle speaks calmly into my ear. "After childbirth, women are in an unusual condition," he says. "Why not have a checkup?"

His hair is no longer blue-black, but his voice never changes.

My husband responds to trouble by increasing his self control. In the hospital corridor he takes my arm with the lightest possible touch. His fingertips are icy.

The obstetrician wears a foolish look on his youthful face. "I only know them from here to here," he explains to someone over his shoulder. His hair is still wet from the swimming pool.

Stripped to the waist, shivering, I lean into the chest X-ray machine. "This is stupid," I think. "It's my head that's killing me. And I don't need any extra radiation."

The nurse was gone. How much time had passed?

In the dark my mother spreads the cushions on the floor.

"I won't leave you," she whispers.

The baby is falling and I cannot catch her. No, she's safe in bed with me. No. She's vanished.

The purple wig bends over me, smelling sweet. "Try this, honey."

The ice. For a moment it dulls the sensation behind my eye, and words begin to tap in my head: "About suffering they were never wrong,/The Old Masters. . . . "

"They haven't found anything yet," said my husband, at his coolest. "They're going to do an EEG today—test your brain waves."

A game show host called from the television: "The question is this. If you could change any part of your body, would it be the top half or the bottom half?"

"Is your hair clean?" said the bored technician. She screwed my scalp full of electrodes, hunched over her table, and dimmed the lights.

"Sleep if you can."

Ballpoint pens scribbled automatically upon a conveyor belt of paper.

"Messages from the spirits," I said.

"Quiet, please."

Lights sparkled in geometric patterns, and I soared into the void.

"I have felt like this before," I thought. "When?"

Every move precise, my husband sets up his camera; the metal petals of the shutter expand and contract; the strobe light multiplies itself on my eyeballs.

In college, I stay up all night to see Janis Joplin at the Fillmore Ballroom. Black air above the dancers seethes with sound, light, smoke. I focus upon a single fixed point to keep my balance as I whirl.

While my father is a graduate student, my little brother starts to spin. He revolves quietly in corners until he is too dizzy to stand. Merely a nervous tic, the pediatrician tells my mother. The habit continues for years. Finally it is replaced by others.

Studying in London I fall ill, but the weather is so bitter, inside and out, that I never feel hot. Instead I have fits of shivering; I compose a long poem about the Underground. But when I wake in my dim rented room, the words melt away. I am not a great poet, after all.

"I have a fever," I said out loud.

"I'm testing," said the technician brusquely.

The fever, they decided, was insignificant. The auger continued to grind at my skull. My mother brought the baby to me, and she tangled her hands in my hair and cried. My scalp was covered with small scabs.

"The EEG is normal," my husband said.

Grease dribbled through two kitchen strainers on the TV screen.

I carried the baby to the window. The hospital was one of a row of blue medical monoliths rising above the north Texas prairie, which was tiled with tiny houses. An occasional steeple jabbed up among them: one had a clock face marked with black Roman numerals and the words, "Night Cometh." No mountains, no canyons. I was homesick for the far West. The sky was wide enough here, however, and perfectly clear.

Dallas was trapped in a heat wave. For fifty consecutive days the temperature had passed a hundred degrees, without rain. Deep cracks opened in the clay beneath the singed lawns, and people stumbled into them.

The maternity ward lay somewhere beneath us. I did not know the name or number of the floor where I stood.

Their eyes glittering, their hair glued into rich curls, two men in white dress shirts hurled an inert body onto a bed and crept off. Organ music rippled from the television.

Time collapsed like folded paper. My mother must have taken the baby away. My husband sat in the dark beside my bed, watching a musical comedy. A Chinese princess and a Renaissance nobleman performed a love duet in a ruined pagoda.

"Marco. . . . " she sang.

And he answered, "Polo. . . . " His lips did not synchronize with the music.

"After the CAT scan tomorrow," said my husband, without expression, "we're calling in another doctor."

"What kind?"

"A psychiatrist."

"No!" I shouted. So I was in the psycho ward. "I'm not crazy. There must be a cause."

The deer hang in the juniper tree. Inverted images: the quick and the dead.

The mesas are on the move. They cruise over my shadow. "Basin and range topography," says my father, gesturing. We travel from house to house, each full of rocks, maps, transits, and magnetometers. A pill bottle of uranium, yellow and lumpy as dry mustard, remains forgotten in the medicine cabinet for many years.

Among the specimens in my father's mineral collection are an Allosaurus vertebra and a chunk of its femur. They are radioactive. The dinosaur's organic material has been replaced by high-grade uranium ore.

Madame Curie derived her radium from fossil wood from Utah.

*Trepan*—in mining, a rock-boring tool used for sinking shafts. In surgery, a trephine.

*Trephine*—a surgical tool with circular serrated edges for cutting out disks of bone, usually from the skull.

My brother finds school difficult but shows a gift for mechanics. At ten, wearing a homemade parachute, he jumps off the roof and breaks his leg.

I have a gift for standardized tests. I write short-lived poems. I begin to travel on my own.

My brother drives an old school bus to Oregon and lives in it, repairing small engines and skydiving.

I graduate, I marry. My Navajo rugs look barbaric in the Dallas house, but after all I have never stayed anywhere for long.

I am pregnant.

The baby's body is born with a rubbery wriggle. The obstetrician duly says, "It's a girl," and turns her around. The faces of several relatives in extremis look back at us before dissolving into her own.

There was no real pain in all of that. Now *this* was a territory I did not know. Then I recognized the bare feet plodding below the hem of the hospital gown.

"You have dull feet," my husband used to tease.

Square, thick, they matched my hands. They looked like my father's. They stopped.

DANGER AREA

Birdless night country.
Outer space. No stars.
Travel at your own risk.
Major test underway.
Some will not get out alive.
Blood will be drunk.
No clues.

"Are you allergic to fish?" asked the young male technician.

"No, why?"

"We inject radioactive iodine dye. When it reaches your brain, we take pictures."

Words drummed: "O the mind, mind has mountains; cliffs of fall/ Frightful . . . ."

"Lie still."

The machine clamped me in its white enamel jaws. I lay alone in an underground chamber while a voice quacked through a perforated metal plate in the ceiling.

"CAT scan? CAT scan? Are you there?"

The machine clicked gently.

Pure blankness. I woke with the same chrome piston apparently pounding my left eye. Where was I? "*Untrumra monna hus*," came the answer. The Anglo-Saxon poet Caedmon, dying, was carried to the "unhealthy men's house." He held my hand. "About suffering—" I began. I saw that he wore a Rolex watch.

"What number between one and ten did I just trace in your palm?" asked the neurologist.

"Seven," I said.

He waved a tiny vial beneath my left nostril. "What do you smell?"

"Nothing."

He moved it to the other nostril.

"Flowers," I said.

"I'm taking myself off this case," said the neurologist.

For the first time a nurse brought me a paper frill, like a nut cup at a children's party, filled with colored pills. She sat on the bed while I swallowed them.

"Did you know," she said, "that this was the hospital where they brought J. R. Ewing on *Dallas* when he was shot?"

Encircled by rings of pink and periwinkle paint, her eyes rose hopefully to the TV screen. A middle-aged man peered through a barred window. "I've got to get out of here somehow," he muttered. In a garden below him another man prowled with a machine gun in his hands.

My husband said, "You have a brain tumor. They found it with the CAT scan. They're calling it a benign meningioma, but we won't know for sure until after the operation."

"I'm not crazy?"

"We told the psychiatrist to go away. You'll like the surgeon."

I dug my fingers into his familiar shoulders. His upper body, usually so calm and set at a lower temperature than my own, was shaking.

"Don't cry," I said. "I'm happy."

I went into surgery as to a bridegroom, washed and exalted. Saying good-by, faces loomed up in a mist: husband, father, mother, and baby. I reached for her fuzzy head and fell back. The big nurse with the purple wig was taping my wedding ring to my third finger.

The neurosurgeon slit my scalp from ear to ear. He sawed a two-inch hinged square from my skull, lifted up the frontal lobe of my brain, and removed the tumor. Then he reassembled my head with wax, thread, and staples.

I watched opaque waves as they divided and rose into crests, precipices, watersheds. There was no smell of mud. I was staring through a row of bars. A green bottle floated up to my mouth.

"Oxygen, ma'am?"

"Yes, please."

The ferry docked, and I put the dark river behind me. My head, half shaved, was wrapped in gauze, harsh to the touch.

"Lady Lazarus," I said.

Nurses unplugged me from various plastic tubes; I sat up, solid and ravenous.

"You're leaving ICU now, sugar. Good luck."

On the regular surgical floor, rings, chains, and a triangle jingled above my bed, as though gymnastic exercises would be required.

"On the day of your operation," said my brother on the telephone from Oregon, "I went skydiving and made a special jump for you."

"Thank you." My throat ached, but still I had not produced one tear. "Be careful, Icarus."

"Me? What about you?"

Making rounds the neurosurgeon bent his wide pink face over his work and admired it. He moved in an atmosphere of Panama hats and white linen suits.

"Benign meningioma, just as I thought," he said, gratified. "Before the CAT scan, we used to operate blind."

"Or lock madwomen up," I thought.

There should be no further problems, he told us. He had scraped the bone clean. He might have been a Southern country lawyer or a gourmet butcher. "Of course I did have to take the left olfactory nerve. But that's why they come in pairs."

I buried my nose in the baby's neck. Newborn, she'd had an acrid yeasty smell, but now it was insipid baby lotion and sour milk. I saw my cranium, an ivory artifact in a glass case.

"But why did it happen?" said my father.

"Who knows?" said the surgeon. "Pregnancy makes everything grow. But the tumor had to be started first."

"When she was three," said my mother thoughtfully, "she had a concussion in just that spot."

"Head trauma!" The surgeon brushed it away. His hands seemed too bulky for his job. "Everyone has head trauma."

"What causes tumors?" I said.

He paused in the doorway, impatience now reducing his dignity. "Oh, genetics. Viruses. Radiation. Who knows?" He relented slightly. "Studies do show more mutations in populations near the equator. Sun."

"It doesn't matter," said my husband with finality.

From this window the ground was much closer; the details of houses and cars and quivering leaves were rich and sharp. A mass of moist clouds had bubbled up in the sky. Behind my back the others went on talking.

"The bone will regenerate," my mother said. "I've seen fossil skulls that had been trepanned and then grew back, partly."

"I wanted to give up," my husband said. "Once I even went to the telephone to call someone, to resign. But who do you call when you want to give up? Everyone was depending on me. So I came back."

That night I could not sleep.

"Nurse—nurse—nurse," called the old woman across the hall, but nobody ever came.

I turned the television volume very low and huddled at the foot of my bed. Doomed lovers moved in triangular patterns. Parents betrayed their children, children their parents. Natural disasters rained down, followed by war. There was a short spell of hope, but at the end a woman lay sick in a thunderstorm. They found her in the morning, her hungry infant nuzzling at her cold breast.

I hugged my own knees. The hospital breathed painfully around me, and I tried to hush my rude joy.

A cylinder soared across the screen and burst, red, white, and blue. It was a giant beer can.

We would camp in remote places, I thought. We were still young. Together we would see orange cliffs, hot blue sky. The baby could ride in a backpack. We would get sunburned and muddy. We would sleep like the dead under the stars. The North Rim, I thought, Canyonlands, Bryce, Zion.

# The Kill

In Montana he used to imagine "back East" as a larger place than this. Now he wonders where the sky has gone, why the colors seem fogged, and how these people have lived for so long with their elbows in each other's faces. Standing, he can easily lay the palm of his hand flat upon the ceiling of his room. The exposed beams still show the marks of an adze, and here and there initials have been carved, then covered with layers of varnish. Over by the fireplace, which is bricked shut, he reads the date 1879.

He lets his arm fall and moves to the window. The old glass shimmers full of flaws, like the surface of a very calm lake. Down near the sill he finds a flattened bubble shaped like the head of a lance. Leaves descend lightly from the elm outside, occasionally pausing for a spin or a glide but always obedient to gravity in the end. On campus, classes are changing. He waits until the bell stops clanging and the interwoven lines of people have hurried away. Then he flings up the sash, leans out the window, and savors the sharp air and the solitude. At home in Montana it is elk season.

He leans from the window for a long time, letting the room grow cold behind him. This will annoy his roommate, who is a freshman, too, but from Long Island. Though neither soft nor fat yet, he gives the impression of overfilling his skin, his pink Oxford cloth shirts, his chino trousers, and his yachting shoes.

The roommate was already entrenched in the better half of the room when the young man from Montana first arrived.

"My God!" exclaimed the roommate. "What the hell is that?"

"A rifle."

"You brought a *gun* to college?"

"Well, it's not a gun. It's a rifle."

"Jesus!"

Apart from a battered car left reluctantly with his brother, the rifle was his most valuable possession.

As he unpacked that day, he could hear voices and excited laughter down the hall. Then his new roommate burst back into the room and announced: "You can't keep it here. There's a regulation. You have to put it in storage."

The Montanan did not realize then how many long blank looks would be required of him.

"Okay," he said.

Instead he hid it under his bed.

He closes the window with a bang and runs downstairs, through the brown gloom of the lobby and off across the ivy-muffled campus, scaring squirrels. He does not remember which afternoon class he is cutting. Down by Lake Carnegie he knows where there are some patches of forest, almost wild except for the muddy path worn through them. He follows it slowly, looking for a stone to skip across the still water but finding none.

"A country without rocks," he thinks, disgusted.

He straddles a fallen tree, frilled with yellow fungus, and watches seven Canada geese fly overhead. Small but clear, their cries come to his ears, and he kicks a clod of mud into the lake violently.

There is a crash in the underbrush ten feet away. The young man stares at the fattest buck he's ever seen. For the space of several heartbeats they watch each other; then the animal takes cover and the man releases his breath. Listening carefully he determines the deer's direction and tracks it briefly, until he finds himself in someone's back yard.

It is a faculty neighborhood: tasteful houses with lake views. He knows this because his freshman English teacher lives nearby, though not in a house because he is merely an assistant professor. He and his wife rent an apartment in a red brick building with a few tricycles on the lawn. The Montanan ducks through a rose garden to a winding road and gets his bearings.

The English professor is a man of frail appearance—a Southerner and a poet, as he declares to the class with a touch of truculence. He seems to be able to switch his Alabama accent on and off like an actor. The class sits around a heavy scarred table in a seminar room that reminds the freshman of his first school in rural Montana, a Victorian structure long since condemned. Here, too, the chalk deposits of decades have turned the blackboard gray; the transom windows refuse to open; the wooden floor is full of groans. The marble stairs, worn into hollows, are somewhat treacherous. As he climbs them the freshman always thinks of drops of water falling upon stone.

"How do you read a poem?"

On the first day of class the professor sprang the question. The students jumped perceptibly. With the gesture of an orchestra conductor, the teacher stabbed his finger at the Montanan, and the young man blurted out the truth.

"As quick as possible—like killing a snake!"

The class rustled in shock and amusement, but the English teacher laughed until tears glittered in his pale blue eyes. He had soft, fair hair like a child's, and a nearly invisible mustache, and he let out little screeches when he laughed. The students uneasily watched him recover his composure.

"Yes," he said at last, wiping his eyes with the back of his hand. "Yes, you're right, poetry's dangerous."

After class he ambushed the young man, who was hoping to get away unnoticed, and apologized.

"I wasn't laughing at you. The idea just tickled me."

Later, after reading an essay about the rifle under the bed, he invited the freshman home for a cup of coffee. It was served by the professor's wife, also thin and blond, but silent while he discoursed in his heaviest accent, which he took up as an instrument of drama, intimacy, or sarcasm.

"We're both outlanders, outlaws, to these Yankees. But y'all wouldn't call them Yankees in Montana, would you?"

"Easterners."

The professor nodded and lit another cigarette. The freshman had never met people who smoked as much as these two. He turned to the woman, who, he guessed, was younger than her husband though still probably almost thirty.

"And you, ma'am?"

"Oh, she's from New York."

The woman smiled faintly and continued to listen with the attentiveness of a note-taker. The freshman felt that man and woman, South and East, were equally alien to him. His professor was talking about food.

"String beans, now, when they are properly cooked—plenty of pot liquor, a ham hock, and okra—and fresh cornbread, never sweet, on the side. . . ."

His wife began to clear away the cups.

"What about girls?" asked the professor.

The young man shrugged, embarrassed. Most of them wanted to be called "women," and they impressed him as females of the same species as his roommate. They had smooth, plump bodies and surprisingly loud voices in class.

"Now," he asked himself uncomfortably, "how do I get out of here?"

The professor's wife rose, and the freshman seized his chance.

"Thanks. Good-bye. See you in class."

And he was off, not quite sure whether it was the sound of laughter or raised voices that followed him down the stairs.

Today he retraces his steps. He is so excited about seeing the buck that he must tell someone. His curious success in English has continued, particularly with a story about an old cowboy who fell into a creek at Thanksgiving and wasn't discovered till he thawed in the spring. The Montanan finds himself admiring the expert way his teacher dissects a poem and identifies the parts. With an effort he remembers that this is not the afternoon for English class, so his professor may be home.

"Where are the kids who own these toys?" he wonders as he crosses the lawn. The brick face of the apartment house gives no clue; every window is hung with the same yellowed Venetian blinds. From somewhere comes the irregular beat of a typewriter.

One night in early October the professor gave a party for the class. As the freshman from Montana was sitting in a corner, balancing his empty glass upon his knee, the professor's wife came up to him. She clutched a green wine bottle by the neck.

"More?"

He shook his head. Then to his amazement she dropped down beside him on the sofa. Her nearness made him go stiff.

"Are you sure?" she asked.

"No thanks. To tell the truth," he stuttered, "I don't like the taste."

She sloshed the bottle at her own glass, which overflowed. White wine drenched her thin skirt, and the freshman stared at the sharp outline of her thigh beneath the wet cloth.

"You'll learn," she said. She raised her glass and drank.

Across the room the professor stood in conversation with one of the young women in the class.

"I was his student, too," remarked his wife.

They watched the professor smile warmly down at the girl.

"I used to write. I had promise, too. I was 'condemned to a life of poetry and poverty.' I wonder if he's telling her that."

The freshman shifted uneasily in his corner. The smell of her moist skin mixed with the smell of the wine—sugar, acid, yeast, and cork—and congested his nose and throat.

"He's published four books since we've been married."

The freshman had never known a person who had written a book before.

"That takes a lot. . . ." she said.

It did not seem to leave a visible mark. Fear swirled around him, and he looked past her toward the door.

The young man rings the doorbell.

"Oh. Hi," says the professor's wife. She is dressed oddly for the daytime, he thinks, in a red kimono carelessly bunched shut at the waist. He observes the bony ridges of her chest and blushes. She stands aside and lets him in.

"What's up?" calls the professor from the next room.

"I'm sorry to bother you—"

"No bother," says the professor easily. As if by reflex both man and woman light cigarettes.

"I just saw a deer! Down by the lake, almost close enough to touch!"

"Did you?" The professor nods, smiling. "Yes, they're real pesky here. They eat people's gardens and multiply uncontrollably. They're protected and quite tame."

"You mean nobody ever hunts?"

"No, Ike. You don't mind if I call you Ike, do you? Someday I'll make you read Faulkner. Though I don't know if anybody who's not a Southerner can ever really appreciate Faulkner."

The woman exhales a veil of smoke and regards both of them through it. The freshman realizes that he is panting lightly.

"I used to hunt," says the professor. "Birds, mostly. And squirrel."

"Squirrel!" exclaims his wife.

"Yes." He looks at her with much the same challenge that he threw to the class when he said he was a poet. "Skinning them is interesting. Like turning a fur glove inside out."

She leaves the room. Her husband turns to his student.

"Would you like a drink or something?"

"No. No thanks."

He moves to the door with decision and heads back across campus at a fast walk. Fortunately his roommate is still out, probably lobbying for admission to one of the exclusive clubs. Working fast, the young man detaches the rifle from the bedsprings, where he has hung it, and breaks it down. The pieces fit under his coat, though they force him to walk rather strangely.

Back in the woods he reassembles the rifle and loads it. He enjoys the feel of it again, the satiny wood and well-oiled steel between his fingers. Then he sits on the fallen tree and waits. By now it is late afternoon, and dusk is settling over forest and water like a shower of soot. Just as the darkness becomes complete the deer slips down to the lake to drink.

At first the young man is afraid that his shaking hands have missed an easy shot. Inadequately dressed, he is cold to the bone, colder than Montana ever made him. And on the edge of a town the noise is dangerous. It does fade, like the repercussions of a pebble in a body of water, and then he hears the buck stumble and fall some distance away.

It is only his third deer and the first he has ever taken alone. Suddenly he hears voices from the houses up above; a flashlight jitters among the trees but soon disappears, and he relaxes. But his hunting knife seems to have lost its edge, and he finds it difficult to work in the dark. At last he manages to clean the animal, half skin it, and carve off a hindquarter. When he stands up, his stiff legs almost buckle. He recognizes the feeling that has been growing inside his chest as dread.

Avoiding the streetlights, he walks to his English professor's apartment. He considers merely leaving the meat on the doormat, but then he remembers his roommate and the rifle.

This time the man opens the door.

"Good God!"

"Venison," says the freshman.

"What have you done?"

"I got the buck. The one I told you about. He was too heavy to carry far, and besides I didn't think about living in the dorm. I can't keep the meat. But he was fat. It should be good eating." The words rattle out, more than he has spoken on a single occasion to anyone since he came to college.

"Come in, you rascal."

The young man lays the hindquarter down on the kitchen table with the hoof sticking over the edge. The professor sinks into a chair and begins to laugh.

"Honey," he shouts. "Come and see what Ike has brought us."

She is still wearing the red kimono. The freshman notices now that it is patterned with large, black, cryptic Oriental characters. Her light hair dangles damply around her face. She catches her breath sharply at the sight in the kitchen.

"Ikey's been a-hunting, a-chasing the deer," cries the professor between little screeches. "Poor dappled fool."

The freshman looks at him doubtfully. He doesn't smell drunk. Then the revelation washes over him: "He *is* laughing at me."

"I can't cook that," the woman raps out, breaking the silence.

"Honey, venison can be delicious."

"I won't."

With new perception the freshman sees that her eyes are rimmed with red and that smoke hangs in the kitchen as in the aftermath of an explosion. He knows that he must go.

"There's just one thing," he begins. "Would you keep my rifle for a day or so? My roommate will—"

The professor hesitates.

"No!" says his wife. "I don't want that thing in my house."

"Just unload it first," says the professor then, in an almost pleasant voice.

"It is."

The young man glances at the woman frozen in the kitchen doorway.

"I'm sorry," he tells her. "I'm really sorry."

He approaches his dormitory, jingling the cartridges in his pocket.

"Jesus Christ." His roommate shrinks backwards in his chair.

In the mirror across the room the Montanan sees himself for the first time. The buck's blood has spattered his coat and stained his hands. There is even a streak across his forehead.

"Are you hurt?"

The freshman from Montana sits heavily on his bed.

"No," he says.

The next time he walks down to the lake it is a brilliant afternoon, so still that the leaves have almost stopped falling, and when they do fall, the crash is noticeable. He whistles quietly as he goes.

"Come back for ol' Betsy?" asks the professor lightly.

The young man nods.

"There she is."

The professor's wife, however, is gone. The freshman wonders what to say, then takes the plunge.

"I'm leaving," he says.

The professor asks what he means. Leaving Princeton?

"I'm just not cut out for the Ivy League. It was a mistake."

"What a shame," says the professor. "Are you sure? What happened? Did you get in trouble over the deer?"

The young man shrugs.

"You're not quitting college altogether, are you?"

"No, I'll probably go back. In Missoula."

"Well." The professor does not observe that his cigarette ash is dropping on the carpet. "I'll miss you. Don't stop writing, now."

"No, sir."

"I wrote a poem about you. It's called 'The Kill.' "

"Maybe I'll read it in a book someday." The freshman zips his gun case shut, feeling that all these words are meaningless. "Please tell your wife good-bye for me."

The professor lifts a hand and lets it fall uncertainly. Afterward he stands at his window for several minutes, watching his student escape.

# A Circle, a Square, a Moon, a Tree

In the Tudor style house live a mother, a father, a teenaged daughter, and two boys about twelve and nine years old.

Lacking a desk, the young woman across the street fans out her papers on the dining table. And then she grimaces as though at an unlucky game of solitaire. She raises her eyes to the window; the Tudor house comes into focus. She knows the family well by sight—their favorite clothes, their habits, their old yellow station wagon—but not by name, and probably she never will. For the street divides the graduate students' apartments, converted army barracks, from the rest of elegant Princeton.

The young woman and her boyfriend were lucky to get an end unit. It is harder to heat but more private than the others, and when she looks through the window behind the table she can almost imagine that she, too, lives in a real house in a comfortable neighborhood. She is often alone, since her boyfriend works at his laboratory while she wrestles with her thesis. When summer comes they will be finished.

She has been observing the family ever since she first moved in, when the children set up a stand in their front yard.

"Look, they're selling blueberries! Shall I buy some for us?"

The berries would burst against her palate and yield small amounts of sweet or sour juice and mealy flesh. Her teeth, after jarring against the seeds and grinding up sugar crystals, would be left faintly marked with purple.

"I don't much care for them."

"Oh. All right."

Later, when the weather turns cold, she sits in a sweater with her dog curled up on her feet and watches a truck deliver fuel oil to the family's furnace. Leaves drop away from the elm and magnolia trees that border the student housing project, and one day a crew of groundskeepers passes slowly under her window, raking and chatting, raking and chatting. Lightweight mountains of dry leaves remain behind them. After school the three children come running through the traffic; the young woman spends an hour watching them play in the leaves. They wade, they fling themselves, they clamber to the top and tumble down with arms outstretched, their concentration relieved by laughter. They are sturdy blond children, not extraordinarily handsome. She perceives a family resemblance in the mauve smudges like lines smoothed by a finger beneath their eyes. The big girl is shy at first, but then her self-consciousness melts and she helps the older boy bury the little one under armloads of red, brown, and orange flakes. He springs out and struts away, clowning.

The young woman laughs. She almost joins them, but some scruple holds her back. When her boyfriend comes home, dinner is late; she tries to explain as she drops the slippery fish into the pan.

"They were having such a wonderful time! But somehow I couldn't approach them. Maybe it would scare them off. They'd know that I was watching them."

"So did they scatter the leaves all over?"

"No, they even piled them back up."

"How's your latest chapter? I finished mine."

"Good for you," she says brightly. The fish, she sees, has stuck to the pan and will fall apart. "Mine's coming."

They are studying different subjects: he, biochemistry; she, history. At first everything about the other was rich and exotic—his Jewishness, her romantic illusions—but now they are finding conversation hard. She tells herself that this is only because they are each immersed in a thesis and a search for a job. They are discovering, however, that their best job prospects are in different places.

A few weeks before Christmas they are both at work in the apartment for once. He has a desk in the bedroom because her typing distracts him. At the dining table she copies and recopies the title of her thesis: "The Lives of Women in a Colonial Village, The Lives of Women—"

"Look!" she calls.

He comes and stands behind her. "What is it?"

The people across the street. They're putting up Christmas lights."

The Tudor house is heavily landscaped, including a pair of small copper beeches, an elm, and an imposing fir tree twenty-five feet tall. Under a steel-gray sky the father of the family and the two boys begin to lift and wind a long string of lights around the fir tree. It is a suspenseful process, and the students stare, expecting the wires to tangle, the ladder to tip, a child to fall. But everything goes slowly and without incident, at a dreamlike pace. The young woman feels her boyfriend's hand on her neck in a caress that is unusual for him.

"They haven't quarreled once," he says at last in a wondering tone.

He classifies everyone immediately as either a Jew or not.

"We have a word for you," he has told her, laughing rather self-consciously.

"I know." Puzzled, piqued, she cannot quite believe that such words have a place between intimates.

And, although she knows it is folly, she can't resist pleading: "Oh, are you sure you can't come home for Christmas with me? You really would enjoy it."

The hand strays away. "I've got to work."

This she thinks is an excuse. In fact she suspects that he will go skiing. But she is willing to be patient, and she drops the subject. She hangs a small wreath on the front door.

As always, her spirits lift at New Year's, carrying her through the blizzards of January and the rejection of a thesis chapter and two job applications. Her boyfriend embarks on a series of promising interviews with a fairly good private college. The thermometer appears to be stuck below freezing, and she wears more and more clothing to bed: a flannel nightgown, socks, then tights. She can hardly remember that last summer she was naked under the sheet. Her boyfriend seems to notice very little change and strides off to his laboratory early in the morning while she copes with frozen pipes.

One Saturday she takes her dog for a walk. The animal, a large rough-coated mongrel, leaps through the snowdrifts as though over hurdles, barking joyously, and the young woman flounders along behind him. She loves the dog, which she adopted last summer and gave a human name, a child's name. As they pass the Tudor house she notices the family departing for the lake with their ice skates, and she almost waves but decides against it. They seem to be a self-sufficient and happy unit; she hesitates to break the shell.

In the mornings, as she dawdles and sorts through her papers, she watches the children leave the house carrying their schoolbooks, followed by the father in the yellow station wagon and finally the mother on foot. When better weather comes the woman begins to ride a bicycle, cautiously, with a brown scarf tied around her pale face. The young woman imagines that the husband is an engineer, the wife a secretary at the university.

The young woman spends hours gazing at the traffic in the street. She begins to recognize both cars and drivers as they pass in the morning and return at night. She watches for an old man on a bicycle, who wears a helmet, a fluorescent orange vest, and a straggling white beard apparently tied up in a net. Each time he flashes by so fast that she almost doubts her eyes. The street runs with little warning into a long narrow bridge, and when she sees a car speed in that direction she sometimes winces. She has smashed the side mirror of her boyfriend's car against the guardrail.

Her boyfriend receives a postdoctoral fellowship.

"How wonderful! Congratulations! Let's celebrate!"

They share the cost of a large pizza and a pitcher of watery beer.

"Of course, a lot depends on grant money," he says and smiles in almost the way she remembers from the beginning. "I'm set for a couple of years anyhow."

She drains her glass down to the bitter soapy foam.

"I wonder if there's anything there for me?" she asks.

In the silence she hears a heavy object hit the floor in the kitchen. A fat dispirited waitress pads by with her tray.

"You can always apply," says her boyfriend. He pries a disk of pepperoni from the remaining pizza and inserts it into his mouth. "But what about Middlebury College? Don't they want you?"

"Nothing is certain yet," she answers. Strings of pinkened cheese are congealing and grease stains are spreading on her paper plate.

"You shouldn't let anything stand in your way."

"But—" She bites off the sentence. An image comes to her mind: a toddler's puzzle or intelligence test with large simple shapes, a circle, a square, a moon, a tree. What he has said is, after all, unanswerable. She still feels hungry but is unable to eat.

The next day she writes sixteen pages, and then the rest of the thesis comes rushing after, six chapters in a month. She passes day after day at the table. Sometimes as she writes she seems to glimpse flashes of movement at the edge of her vision, yet when she looks up she sees nothing but the lawn, the trees, the street, and the Tudor house. She stops cooking, and after working late into the night she often falls asleep on the sofa. As the afternoons draw out, the man across the street begins to rake his lawn after work. He scatters lime and fertilizer; he carefully prunes his hedge.

Listening to the church bells, she works straight through Easter Sunday. Her boyfriend has openly gone on a ski trip over this holiday. He has, he says, only one more chapter to write. In the middle of the morning the family across the street emerges dressed for church. The man wears a sport coat, slightly too tight for him, and his blond crewcut glitters in the weak sunshine. The woman wears a dark conservative dress, the girl an obviously new one. She takes awkward steps on small high heels. The younger son has been subdued by his coat and tie. But where is the other boy? They climb into the station wagon and drive away as she speculates. Perhaps he is also on a trip.

Then one afternoon the young woman opens her door and steps onto the porch. The dog nudges past her and wanders back and forth, his nose pressed to the damp, faded grass. There is a distinct glow in the air. Scarlet tulips bloom across the street. She looks down and notices with a kind of delicious pain that some previous resident of her apartment has dared to plant an extravagant quantity of bulbs. Up against the shabby wall the blossoms jostle one another: lemon-colored daffodils, stiff clusters of hyacinths in artificial tones of pink and blue, paperwhite narcissi, tulips as brilliant as gift wrapping ribbon.

She picks her way gingerly across the thawing mud. Each island of grass squeaks and oozes water when she steps on it. She kneels and buries her head among the flowers.

"What are you doing?"

Startled, she lets out a cry. Her boyfriend has come up quietly behind her. As her heart slows down she reads alarm and guilt in his face.

"I was just smelling the flowers."

Cold muddy water is soaking through the knees of her jeans, and she rises.

"I'm finished," she says, momentarily lightheaded.

"Oh?"

"All through. Except for the typing. I just finished the last chapter—'Childbirth and Mortality.' " She watches him draw back somewhat. She is aware that his regard for her work is low.

After a moment he says lightly, "What, no conclusions?"

"Already done."

"Well. Great."

They move unconsciously towards the door. She considers scratching his face or falling at his feet. But instead she hears herself say in an unfamiliar, choking voice: "I'm worried about something."

"What?"

"The people across the street. There used to be two boys, but now there's only one."

His eyes follow her gesture. The father, in his customary red and black mackinaw, is repainting his front door while the small boy watches. He holds a baseball which from time to time he tosses up in the air and catches, *cloc*.

"How do you know he's gone?"

She shrugs impatiently. "I haven't seen him. When they go out, it's only the four of them."

"Maybe he was just a vistor."

She shakes her head. "He looked like them."

"Maybe he's on a trip. Foreign exchange student or something."

"He was too young."

"So he was a cousin. Or just happened to look like them. Or got mixed up with drugs and ran away. Or isn't gone, in fact. Maybe you're wrong. You don't really know them, do you? So why care?"

A miserable sensation begins again, as though all the bones in her chest are crushed and grating against one another. Surprised, she realizes that it had stopped while she knelt in the grass.

Typing is a simpler task than writing, but it leaves less time to stare out the window. She tries to lose herself in margins and footnotes. When she does look up, she sees her boyfriend's footprints on the ground outside. After weeks of sun they now resemble impressions in iron. She, treading on the grass, has left no mark at all.

Early one evening in May the girl across the street comes out in a long yellow silk dress. With her blond hair she reminds the young woman of one of the daffodils now dried to onion skin in the garden beneath the window. The girl spins, taking a child's delight in her gown, and her mother appears behind her. Together they walk down the street to a neighbor's house to show off the dress. The girl is preoccupied with holding up her skirt; the mother occasionally puts out a protective hand.

"The prom," whispers the young woman at the window.

She remembers a tinfoil moon slowly rotating above a dance floor. It is perhaps unfortunate, she thinks, that the girl resembles her father so much.

She carries her typescript to the thesis bindery ahead of her boyfriend after all. But she still has no job. After Commencement, if all else fails, she will go home. She starts to pack, separating her things from his without comment. He writes furiously at the desk in the bedroom.

"Oh!" she gasps.

"What?" he says sharply.

"The tree—the tree."

"What *is* it?"

She points. "They're cutting down the fir tree."

The father is armed with an orange chain saw. While the rest of the family stands by, he pulls the starter and attacks the fir tree. A hideous noise rattles the neighborhood, and the mother covers her ears with her hands.

The two children are fascinated. Soon the tree begins to waver and then crashes onto the lawn at an angle to the Tudor style house. Like multiple dark green wings, its branches continue to vibrate for some time before they grow still. The chain saw is mercifully shut off.

"If a tree falls in the forest, does it make a noise?" asks her boyfriend flippantly. "Of course not."

The young woman bursts into tears.

"What's the matter with you?"

"Why didn't I see an ambulance? If there was a funeral, why didn't I know?"

She runs blindly into the bathroom, where the only window is high and opaque, and she slams the door.

"God!" he says.

She understand that he will not, cannot comfort her.

A few weeks later, there is a very little left to do. Commencement is over; her rented cap and doctor's gown have been turned in. Her former boyfriend has left before the ceremony. Soon her parents will arrive to collect her, the last of her belongings, and the dog. At the last moment she has gotten a second-rate job far away on the West Coast. She feels anesthetized, glad to be alone. The shadows and flashes have mostly disappeared from the edge of her vision. Out of habit as she passes the window she looks across the street.

The children are selling blueberries again. But this year only two figures sit behind the stand.

She wonders suddenly if he ever existed. When she goes closer, however, she sees that these are quite solid, sunburned, and ordinary children. Their square white teeth are stained with purple. She averts her eyes from the raw tree stump.

"How much a basket?"

"Fifty cents," answers the girl shyly, and the small boy pushes one forward.

She wants to ask other questions. Who are you? Where is he? What happened? Why? But the children do not speak, and neither does she. She takes up the basket of precariously balanced berries and examines the flattened globes of navy blue, frosted with silver. She carries them carefully through the traffic. She thinks that at least some of them will be sweet.

# Marble

"Where are we going?" the child asked.

His mother untangled his small arms from the straps of the car seat. The pickup truck shuddered and stopped.

"No shade," said her husband. "I guess we'll park here."

"What's this?" said the child.

She murmured vaguely to him and opened the door into a tide of hot air. The Arizona sun drove over their exposed bodies. Its first touch was luxurious; then the young woman's scalp began to prickle with sweat.

"One, two, three—jump!" Clinging to her hands, the little boy hurtled from the truck. He stamped his sandals in the pinkish dust and squealed with pleasure.

"Again. Again!"

"No. . . ."

She had caught sight of an oval photograph of a woman, a picture that had the quality of a mug shot or passport photo. The subject was in her late middle age, and the unkind light had turned her hair into some sharp inky thing, her face into craters and mounds. Her eyes were dull.

The young woman drew in her breath and glanced at her husband. He was standing absolutely still, arms at his sides, as was his habit, watching her. His sunglasses were so dark that she could not fully understand his expression.

"Let's go," he said.

"Where are we going?"

She answered, "To see some big rocks. This is a rock store." Her husband swung the child up to sit on his shoulders, and she continued in a lower voice, "Was that picture—?"

"I think so."

In spite of the heat, chills radiated from the center of her back. For many years she had driven past this place and wondered what mysteries the rambling sheds and windowless office concealed. After five o'clock at night the whole business was locked up in a wrought iron palisade, and she imagined that a guard dog spent the nights inside. Warily she stepped through the gate. But the yard appeared to be deserted, and her husband lifted their son down. The child immediately trotted off. He still ran clumsily, just pumping his legs from the knees down, but he was fast.

"John," she called. "Stick around."

She had to go and catch him. Dodging back and forth, he howled first in glee and then annoyance as she took his hand.

"What's this, Mommy?"

"A tombstone," she said as casually as possible. Of course he was hardly more than a baby, happy with the simplest answers. Perhaps she should have said, "A rock." But one of her own clearest memories of childhood was the certainty that adults were keeping fearful secrets. Surely it was best to be frank if she could, she told herself, and led him towards the office.

"What's that?"

"Another tombstone."

John had wandered into a display or storage area, through which they now threaded their way. It was a flat sandy expanse divided by a long driveway, and the finished stones were set out in tidy rows. The driveway ran into a busy street. Beyond the traffic loomed the cemetery, cool, green, dark, and deep, its well-fed trees thrusting high into the burnished sky. In the black shade beneath them, grave markers showed up like a collection of teeth. She saw her husband disappear through a door labeled "Marble/ Granite/ Monuments" and felt a flicker of irritation.

"Come on, honey. It's hot here."

Instantly he lagged.

"Look, numbers," he said.

"Yes," she agreed. "And letters."

She realized that she'd been avoiding the inscriptions, but this one forced itself upon her: "Howard Westfall, 1897–1980." Not bad, she thought; a long life and a beautiful rock. It was a wedge, speckled black and white with one face polished to the texture of wet paint and the others left artfully rough. The term "rusticated stone" bobbed to the surface of her mind, probably a survivor from one of her art courses. She was uncertain, however, whether the rock was granite or marble.

John slipped away and she followed him more slowly, reading every word she passed, as though in some kind of penance. "Jesús G. García, 1918–1981." "Patricia Mitchell, 1935–1978." Simple, clean, and undeniable as they were, they made her feel ashamed of being squeamish.

"When did I first understand it?" she thought, and then remembered.

Aged three, she had been standing beside her mother in the kitchen. "Everybody? Me too?"

"Yes," her mother said.

She could still feel the rush of terror and grief.

"But not for a long, long time," her mother added quickly.

Warm relief came flooding in, but it did not cancel her knowledge.

Another memory dropped into place behind the first one: how she had loved her slender, patient grandfather. He walked to his iron bed for a rest prescribed in the middle of the day; the children were not supposed to bother him then. She stood in the doorway watching him go.

"Of course," she thought. "It happened when I was three. That's why I was asking her."

She glanced at the stone at her feet. "Marilyn Jean O'Reilly, 1947–1977." Only thirty, she saw with a start, and quickened her pace after her son. He had stopped to finger a white tablet, one of half a dozen propped in a wooden rack.

"Look, Mommy, a star."

In fact it was a star of David. In the next row she observed a tombstone carved with Oriental characters; the swooping lines were stiffened and blunted by the chisel.

"Let's go inside where it's cool."

"No." He danced away again like a little boxer. By this time they had reached partial shade. A porch roof made of thin slats went jutting out from the main building and threw stripes over the gravestones and urns that rested nearest the door. She reached for the knob and called, "Daddy's waiting."

"Shoes, Mommy!"

A life-size sculpture of baby shoes topped a thick white monument nearly as tall as John. "Our Little Angel" began the inscription, but she picked up her child and turned away, stern and embarrassed, without finishing it.

After the glare outside, the musty office seemed as dark as a closet. They blinked. On one edge of a large desk spread with papers, a young woman in blue jeans was eating her lunch.

"Well, *hi*," she cooed to the little boy, who turned his face towards his mother's neck.

"We're in here, Laura." Her husband appeared in an open doorway connecting the first office to another.

"A dog," said the child.

All his mother saw was a row of mismatched chairs pushed against the wall, and a large quantity of cards, notices, and yellowed clippings tacked up above them. A faint growl came from one of the chairs.

"That's Rosie," said the girl, rattling the crushed ice in her cup.

An old black poodle raised its head, then let it fall again. Curled up in a black armchair, it was barely visible.

"Rosie! Quiet!" shouted a deep voice from the next room.

There, squeezed behind another large desk, they found the possessor of the voice: surprisingly, a female. She was a gigantic woman, obese but as firm as the belly of a horse.

"Ah! You've got a say in this, don't you, sugar?"

Laura smiled stiffly and released the little boy, who ran to his father.

"My wife is an artist."

"Ah!" said the fat woman again, with a hearty lack of interest. Her original fairness was vastly swollen and coarsened; she was past fifty. Yet she still had the sandy curls of a handsome young man. "You paint pictures? Or are you a decorator?"

In the gloom high above the desk hung a stuffed sailfish. The effect of the taxidermy had been curious. All traces of living color and texture were gone, replaced by flamingo and aqua glazes reminiscent of the cheap plastic of the early Fifties. Only the fish's own size and shape remained.

Laura's husband prompted her. "She's a sculptor."

"Just a potter really. I've only worked in clay, not stone." And done nothing for years, she added silently, looking at her husband with a mixture of shame, rage, and love.

"Well, honey," said the fat woman, "go and find you a nice piece of marble for your redecorating. I've told *him* all about it. Everything we got is out back. Just look around."

"Is this unusual? How much stuff do you sell that's not for tombstones?" The young man tickled his son, looking sideways at the fat woman. "I guess *that* business is steady," he joked.

The fat woman shrugged, bored. "Oh, we sell a lot," she said. "Windowsills. Fireplaces. Roman baths. What is it you want? Kitchen counters?"

"No," said Laura. "Just a small slab."

"Well, you go look around. You'll excuse me not coming; I can't take the heat. These are the dog days."

They walked through a showroom paved with samples of various stones. The classic frosty white of goddesses and pillars lay beside a range of other colors.

"Gaudy," Laura said.

Her husband nodded. "Looks artificial, doesn't it?"

A sliding door opened directly into the rock yard, where a workman in a rubber apron and goggles was operating a huge saw. As he worked, the machine roared and a stream of cloudy water flowed over the rock under treatment, down past the man's feet, and away along a shallow ditch to a puddle rich with mud. Someone had sprinkled white marble chips ineffectually on the wet ground.

"Hot," complained John.

"Would you pick him up, Jack?"

"He's big enough to walk."

"Oh, all right." The heat made her feel detached and passive. She watched her son plow along, setting a foot in all the softest patches of mud. He squatted to collect some pebbles.

"See anything you like?"

Irregular ovals of rock leaned against the main building. They were obviously one-inch slices of boulders. Larger slabs, four feet by ten feet and perfectly angular, had been propped against a high wall that bordered the property.

Laura put out her hand. Even with the air at 107° the rock was cool. She stroked the gleaming surface, finding small flaws where the dark veins ran. The notched edges and reverse sides were harsh.

"I've never seen brown marble before," she said, pointing at another piece. It was an oily walnut color crammed with paler blobs.

"How about green?"

Lush as algae, the colors clustered on the slab. The little boy ran in short dashes around his parents as they inspected more stones: crumbly gray, beige with pockmarks, dull black slate, and pink granite that reminded Laura of glacial Egyptian gods in museums. Some of the specimens were nightmarish, too, the colors of fever dreams, bodily secretions. Dirty yellow oozed into green, and gray swallowed them both.

The most impressive of all was a black marble slashed with glittering white.

"Outer space," Laura said.

Jack looked at her without answering. Perspiration crept over his temples. Black marble was the most expensive, he told her: fifty dollars a square foot.

"It's lovely," she said. "I'll always recognize real marble now."

"What is marble? I used to know." Her husband tapped the brilliant rock thoughtfully. His store of general knowledge was often surprising; in college she had never met a more indifferent student.

"I don't know," she answered, looking away and locating John, who was chucking pebbles into the wastewater.

"Metamorphic. That's it. Marble is made out of limestone by heat and pressure."

"Lime?" she said. "Bones?"

"If you like it, let's get it."

"Oh, I don't know."

Sometimes she wished that they still lived in their first shabby apartment, with their possessions in cardboard boxes and her clay on the kitchen table. She seemed to have dwindled since then. Of course, there was the baby now.

The spectacle of marble stirred her old interests in an almost painful way. Michelangelo, she remembered, had called his marble *carne*. Flesh. Meat. The shape lived inside the stone, or some such thing, and he merely dug it out. This explanation had always struck Laura as coy, but suddenly she understood: she saw life forms crushed into rock.

Jack shaded his eyes, and she watched a certain long muscle flex in the hollow of his cheek. It was a sign of strain.

"Where's John?" she said.

He was no longer standing by the puddle. The machine roared and sang against the stone, the water poured, the sun blurred their vision.

"John? Johnny?"

Together they saw the small shape trotting down the driveway and into the road. He paused in the gutter as a delivery truck, a motorcycle, and an orange car drove past. He took another step forward. Laura began to run, calling to him. Jack stood still but raised his voice to a level that Laura had never heard before.

"John, stop!"

The child froze. Jack shouted again: "Come back!"

Laura lifted him out of the street. After carrying him a few feet, she felt her knees fold, and she leaned against the wall in a pocket of deep shade. Jack came towards them with measured strides. When he put his arms around them, both Laura and John were crying. The little boy sobbed raucously, with high wails, sensing his parents' terror. Laura's skin was cold, and the marble all about them appeared colorless and insubstantial to her.

"Things are very fragile," Jack said.

She could not control her memories. A horde of them descended and choked her: the baby's birth, Jack's amazed expression, and then a tingling sensation. It was not unpleasant. She seemed to be lying beneath a shower of raindrops, infinitely small. Slowly she registered two impressions; Jack's face floated above her, and a needle burned in the tenderest part of her arm. Somewhere, removed and concentrated, there was discord, a jangle without sound. The rain continued to fall. She was quite alone. But now she identified the jangle as pain, and she found herself trapped in a grim contest. Before her eyes a grid was marked with squares in a pattern that presented a choice. She knew that this was a matter of black and white, evil or good, off or on, and desperately significant. Something—what?—must be avoided. Yet every time she made a choice the puzzle on the grid was replaced by a new one. She felt herself losing the struggle. Clutching at certainties, she repeated her own name aloud. Then, when this had no effect, she cried out the names of her husband and son: "Jack and John, Jack and John." She knew that they would not come; the words were merely a charm to hold off the enemy.

The combat was ended, and she felt herself skimming along feet first, as though she lay in an open boat. Great fumy avenues or waterways opened in the darkness before her, powdered with points of light, tempting her with exquisite ease. Nothingness. It was simple, it was familiar, it was, after all, completely safe.

But another word began to irritate her mind: "infection." At first it was meaningless; finally it reminded her of something suspended just out of reach. She opened her eyes, and a stranger told her that she was almost well, and so was the baby. The man's face, above his starched white coat, was as brown and evenly rifted as a dried mud puddle.

"We thought we were going to lose you both," said the doctor, dropping his professional mask for a moment.

Laura curled up sideways in her narrow metal bed and wept effortlessly.

"Things are very fragile," Jack said.

Now she perceived warmth trickling back into her fingers. Pandemonium had melted away. For over two years she had fought these attacks; they left her dull and hollow. She felt like a person who walks to a familiar well, drops a stone, and hears nothing.

"I let him wander, I let him wander." she berated herself.

Jack said, "Let's decide on the black marble, and go."

Laura picked up her son's smooth hand, which twisted away from her. John was not a baby anymore.

"I don't want black," she said calmly. "Give me five more minutes."

At the back of the yard she discovered a small slab of white marble, perfect, she thought, for its place in her new kitchen.

"What'll it be?" asked the fat woman.

The chairs in her office were wide and half-sprung. Laura touched John's silky scalp and looked up at the stuffed sailfish, thinking of the bereaved people who had sat there before her. Jack attempted to bargain.

"Are you a contractor?" The fat woman peered over her pink plastic glasses.

He said he was an engineer who did his own contracting.

"Well, we have only one price anyhow," she answered. "That's the best Carrara marble."

"I'm thirsty, Mommy."

"Water in the workroom," said the fat woman, gesturing with her elbow. "These are the dog days."

They found an old-fashioned water cooler with a stack of white paper cones to drink from. Several gray stone tablets, already incised, had been laid out upon a rough table, and the girl from the front office was painting them.

"See the pretty pictures?" she asked John.

The Virgin of Guadalupe bore red roses and a golden crown; Jesus' halo glowed. It was a double tombstone: "*Querida madre . . . Estimado padre . . . Que descansen en paz.*" The girl was applying green paint to another stone, and she leaned aside with a giggle while Laura read:

> You go your way and I'll go mine,
> High and low, rain or shine,
> And if the two should chance to meet,
> Grass will be green and wine taste sweet.

On either side of this epitaph was carved a large marijuana leaf. As Laura marveled, half amused and half repelled, she noticed the girl's curly hair.

"Why, they're mother and daughter," she thought.

Across the hall the hoarse voice warned, "We always take payment in advance."

Jack asked when the slab would be ready.

"Can't say for sure." The fat woman suddenly unreeled a couple of paper towels from a roll on her desk and mopped her forehead and jowls. "Feels like a storm's coming, and the men don't work in the rain. They might get electrocuted. These are the dog days, aren't they?"

A Mexican workman, pale with dust, stared after them mutely as they left.

Laura laid the ball of dough upon the slab and began to roll it out. Stroke by stroke she flattened it, watching the circle of pastry cover the patterns in the marble. A dim unhappiness hung over her.

"Mommy, what are you doing?"

"Cooking," she said absently.

The child threw his arms around her knees and gripped them until they ached.

"We'll have a little reception—afterwards," Laura's mother had told her.

"Just cake and coffee. And could you bring a pie? You make such good apple pies."

Laura remembered her great-aunt's sharp voice, dismissing the bad grades of some girl cousin. "Oh, don't worry about *her*. She'll get married and make pies."

Granular, greasy, and unappetizing, the dough lay in a ragged mat. Laura's fingers moved automatically. And after all, she thought, what had her great-aunt done with her life? Run a ranch? Feuded with her neighbors? Laura gathered up the scraps of pastry and idly decorated the top crust. Excellent, she decided. In fact that trim would work well in clay; she could clearly see it glazed and fired. But a new thought rose and punctured her satisfaction.

"Black," she said aloud. "Black marble would be better, after all."

Autumn had arrived all at once, and under the thick Aleppo pines and cypress trees—the tallest in town—the mourners shivered. Laura's great-aunt had outlived her husband, child, old enemies, and friends, but still a large crowd stood by her grave. Dictatorial as always, she had arranged every detail for herself. "They did the best they could," read the epitaph. The double headstone only lacked the final date.

"Marriage," thought Laura, barely hearing the words of the priest.

Once she had seen the statues of an Etruscan couple stretched out embracing upon their tomb. She yearned for Jack, but he had been reluctant to come. Her eye skipped down the strata exposed by the open grave: torn grass, soil, and the pale pinkish sand of the desert, choked with rocks.

A gust of wind came sweeping through the trees and sifted a very fine rain down upon the funeral.

Laura lifted her face. Drawing her jacket tight, she stood alone, waiting. But miraculously this time the claws did not descend. Beneath her fingers a hard young torso breathed; the pain below her ribs was only hunger.

# Lavinia Peace

*The girl's eyes are pale brown, enormous, and grave. She wears a straw hat trimmed with daisies. Long brown hair tumbles past her shoulders. The hat is also pale brown, like the daisies.*

"There she is!" said Lynn.

"In the back row?" asked Catherine.

Silent for a moment, the sisters heard silverware jingle against china. Their mother and Lynn's husband were cleaning up after Christmas dinner. Lynn's two children rode their new bicycles in gleeful circles on the patio outside.

*In front of the girl, a man with a heavy mustache sits in one Victorian armchair, a woman with a lace cap in the other. She holds a baby in a long dress. Other children sit crosslegged in a semicircle on the brown grass. A substantial brown brick house rises in the background.*

"Eight children," Catherine marveled.

"Lavinia was the oldest," said Lynn, finding that it was fun to instruct her own older sister, for once. "She's about seventeen here." Delicately she lifted the faded sepia photograph.

"Lavinia Peace Merton," said Catherine, deciphering the spidery handwriting on the back.

"Our great-grandmother."

"Peace?"

"She was born in London on the day the Crimean War ended," Lynn explained. Then she looked at Catherine with surprise and a stab of familiar envy. "You can read that handwriting? It took me weeks."

"I can't believe how much work you've done," Catherine said.

Lynn wondered if Catherine were sincere. Years ago they had never had the same interests; Catherine lived in the present moment, or perhaps the future. Yet after the plum pudding was eaten ("One big greasy raisin!" laughed Catherine) and the coffee drunk, their mother had urged Lynn to show her sister the family papers, and Catherine had seemed eager.

Catherine added, "Did you learn how to do this at library school?"

"No," said Lynn sharply. Condescending as usual, she thought; Catherine the celebrity, Lynn the drudge. And they had just sat through another meal with Lynn and her mother doing all the work. It would never change.

Then she remembered that this was not the brilliant Catherine who had left the West twenty years ago, swearing never to return: "The stinking desert," she had called it. This was a woman between jobs, with gray in her hair, who had come back to live in her mother's house again.

"We did cover conservation," Lynn said more gently. "Old paper gets yellow and brittle, you know."

She unfolded a printed page.

"Why, it's a concert program," said Catherine. " '*Ave Maria*'—Miss Lavinia Merton, soprano."

"Here she is about that time."

*A woman in her early twenties sits at an angle to the camera, her head tilted. Yards of wavy hair flow over one shoulder and taper away in wisps around her knees. She wears a striped taffeta gown, a locket, and earrings. The expression on her face is serious, almost pleading.*

"Cloth, hair—she's so weighted down," Catherine said pityingly. "Speaking of weighted, dinner was delicious, Lynn, but I ate too much. I'm not used it it."

"What are you used to?" Lynn well remembered a macrobiotic summer, and more recently a regimen of vitamins.

"I eat very little meat," Catherine said with an air of virtue.

There was a lingering, crystalline crash from the kitchen. Lynn sprang up, but her sister held her back.

"Whatever happened, it's over now. Let them take care of it."

Lynn sat again, her guilt overcome by the sight of Catherine's long fingers disarranging the neat piles of papers.

"Lavinia passed the entrance exams for Cambridge University, but her father wouldn't let her go," said Lynn.

Catherine shook her head. "At least that wouldn't happen today."

"Wouldn't it?" Lynn thought of the time that Catherine was arrested in an antiwar demonstration, and how she dropped out of school afterwards. Their parents had refused to send Lynn away to college when her turn came. "But why rake that up now?" she said to herself. "It's Christmas. And I did all right at home, didn't I?"

Catherine discovered that the back of the second picture was blank. "So what did Lavinia do?" she asked.

"Helped with the younger children, probably. Practiced her music. And here's one of her sketchbooks."

*An English thatched cottage, a wood, and a pond. A hammock suspended between two trees. A girl with a fan.*

"Of course she was supposed to get married," Catherine said slowly.

"Well, yes," Lynn answered. "There would have been parties, dances."

Catherine had been involved with many men: boyfriends who took her on dates, college romances, a Frenchman, a Mexican, and two others with whom she lived for years. Her mother was the only one who mentioned marriage, and not lately. Catherine had come home alone.

"Let me show you something," said Lynn.

The slim red leather box was made to fit the palm of a lady's hand. The lid was lined with a mirror. Beneath a white satin pad, nestled on white velvet, were seven objects made of ivory, steel, and gold.

"What is it?"

"An embroidery kit. Thimble, scissors, pincushion, needlecase . . . ."

"Every woman had to sew, I guess?"

Lynn sewed; Catherine didn't.

"Yes, but this was a present," said Lynn.

She pulled out a pair of calling cards. The first was engraved, "Lieut. J. N. Benbow, R.N. H.M.S. *Andromeda*." In a large, clear handwriting, the second read: "Major Merton. For Miss Merton. South Street, Eastbourne."

"And who was Lieutenant Benbow?" asked Catherine.

"Who knows? Not our great-grandfather, though."

How romantic!" Catherine said.

The mirror reflected their faces close together. Misty with age, it softened the difference between Lynn's freckled skin and Catherine's dark coloring, revealing the likeness in the bones.

"How have you learned so much, Lynnie?"

"When Daddy died, Mother cleaned the attic and found these things. She remembers a lot that Gram told her, too." Lynn closed the sewing kit with a snap. "And I've done some research," she said.

She slipped the photograph into a special protective envelope.

"I didn't think you'd care about it," she told Catherine.

History, family, women's concerns—Catherine had always seemed oblivious to them.

"Where's your sister?" people used to ask.

"In the Peace Corps," Lynn would answer. "Graduate school . . . Bolivia . . . working as a journalist . . . living on a farm . . . making a film . . . I'm not quite sure."

Nowadays fewer people asked about Catherine. Lynn had a job and family of her own.

"But I am interested," Catherine protested. "What happened next?"

*Her face is wild. A cowboy hat perches on her tangled hair. His hat is pulled down over his eyes, and a curly mustache hides his mouth. Around his neck he wears a bandanna. He threatens her with a six-shooter. She holds a knife at his throat.*

"She met George," said Lynn.

"But what—"

"Oh, it's a joke picture," said Lynn. "Look close. They're laughing."

"How on earth did Lavinia get from Victorian England to the wild West?"

"George took her."

Lynn laid a yellowed envelope, postmarked June 1893, upon the desk.

*George G. Standish, Esq.*
*Keam's Canyon Trading Post*
*Arizona Territory*
*U.S.A.*

She explained that George was an Englishman who had gone West to look for gold but settled instead as a trader among the Indians in Arizona.

Lynn tipped the envelope and a pink rosebud fell out. Catherine gave a strange little cry.

*My dearest George,*

*I have been trying to sing, but my piano is not in tune, and I am out of tune, without you. So I have decided to write a letter instead . . . .*

"Why, she was thirty-seven," said Catherine, calculating. "My age."

"Yes. They weren't married for three more years, either."

Deep in the letter, Catherine did not reply. The she touched the dry rosebud with the tip of a finger and said, "She must have given up. She was an old maid, surely."

"Yes," said Lynn.

Yet, she went on, at the age of forty Lavinia Peace Merton crossed the Atlantic with her stern father, Major Merton. She married George Geoffrey Standish in New York City at the Little Church around the Corner. She said good-bye to her father, who lingered as long as possible, thinking that she might change her mind. And George and Lavinia boarded a train for Arizona Territory.

There was no wedding picture.

Lynn opened a small gray book and passed it to her sister. Catherine puckered her brow over the words pencilled inside.

*My dear old family,*

*I shall send you this journal when it is filled, to serve as letters home. Everything is glorious. Of course Papa will have told you all about the wedding, and how he saw us off, a few hours ago. Already the scenery is growing rough and picturesque, compared to England, but George only laughs and says nothing compares to the West. I cannot wait. He sends his best love to you all. We have booked a "sleeper" all the way to Albuquerque: such a curious name, but nothing like the Indian words I must now learn, living at the Trading Post on the Moqui Reservation.*

"Once, in Europe," smiled Catherine, "I shared a train compartment overnight with a honeymoon couple."

"I've never been abroad," said Lynn stiffly.

"Why not?" asked Catherine.

That was just like her, thought Lynn indignantly. Catherine had no responsibilities. She could spend all her money on herself. Even now, when she claimed she was bankrupt, she wore newer clothes than Lynn did—huge, flashy things that suited her perfectly.

"If I wore them, I'd look like a child playing dress-up," Lynn thought, sighing.

"She writes that the trading post was three days' journey from town in a buckboard or on horseback," Catherine said.

*The stone house has its back to a cliff. A fragile fence cuts through the sharp, dry weeds where a horse is grazing. On a porch, a small female figure dressed in white is reading a book.*

"Exile," breathed Catherine.

"Keam's Canyon is still isolated today," Lynn said.

"But," said Catherine, leaning forward, "the past wasn't brown and gray like this picture. That sky was bluer than any heaven Lavinia ever imagined. The Arizona dirt is like pigment. Orange mesas, Indian blankets. And she was in love."

"Married," said Lynn, more dully than she intended. Since when, she wondered, did Catherine find Arizona dirt romantic?

"To me the present often seems gray compared with the past," Lynn said.

*Every niche in the Indian pueblo is crowded except for a sandy space in the center. All faces are turned to it. Here, stripped to the waist, stands a man with streaming white hair. The snake in his mouth has writhed into a double S-curve. Above the dancer's head a woman is sitting. The flounces of her skirt fall in tiers over an adobe stairway. Her face has disappeared in the shade beneath her lace parasol.*

"I think that's Lavinia," said Lynn.

"I'm sure it is," said Catherine. "But where's George?"

"Washing the snakes," said Lynn.

*21 Aug. 1896*

*My dearest Papa and Mamma,*

*I must describe the Snake Dance while it is fresh in my mind.*

*It is an annual rain-making ceremony among our neighbors the Moqui. For nine days the Indians collect snakes and carry out rituals. And George, who has become an honorary member of the Antelope Clan, assisted in a kind of Holy Baptism of the reptiles! As they included* deadly rattlesnakes, *I was in terror!*

*But all went well, even when the medicine men danced with the snakes in their mouths! Instantly we had torrents of rain.*

*Naughty George says it's the only practical religion he knows.*

"It wasn't all like that," said Lynn. "Most of her diaries and letters are just about everyday life. Sometimes she was lonely and homesick."

"I like George," Catherine said with relish.

*He lounges in front of a tall fireplace. Flames are not visible, but orange light spills into the shadowy room, lurid upon his hair, his grin, and the human skull in his hand.*

"The devil!"

"At the turn of the century there was a fad for hand-colored photographs like this," said Lynn. "He really did have red hair."

Dusk was falling. The sisters heard Lynn's children come inside, slamming the door behind them and talking in high, strained voices. "Tears before evening," thought Lynn.

She and Catherine looked at a shrunken kid glove, a gold locket, and a worn Book of Common Prayer with Lavinia's name on the flyleaf.

"And this," said Lynn, "is her riding habit."

She held the green woolen costume up to her own body.

"She was tiny," Catherine remarked.

"But see?" Lynn lifted a panel of the skirt.

"She wore pants underneath!" cried Catherine.

They burst out laughing.

"In a while they moved to town," Lynn went on. "Her first baby, our grandmother, was born in 1897."

*The man's hair and mustache look red even in the gray portrait. He faces the photographer with a grin. The woman's large eyes are somewhat tired and guarded, but her hat is set at a jaunty angle, and the frills on her shirtwaist blouse are crisp. One of her hands rests lightly on the shoulder of a small child, faintly blurry.*

"A first baby at forty-one," said Catherine, awed.

"And another three years later. Great-uncle Geoffrey."

*The boy and girl both wear starched dresses and shoulder-length curls. He sits in a velvet chair, his short legs sticking straight out. He is perhaps two years old. Standing beside him, his sister holds an Indian doll carved from wood and decorated with feathers.*

"That's something I'm afraid I'm going to miss," said Catherine after a pause. "I envy you, Lynnie."

The little boy reminded Lynn of her own son. "Is it possible," she thought, "that he'll ever be as old and withered as Uncle Geoffrey?" Could her young daughter die prematurely, far from home?

"There's nothing like it, Catherine," she said .

For good—and bad, she thought. She could hear her children playing now with the extravagant electronic toys that Catherine had given them for Christmas.

"Lavinia had rheumatic heart disease," she said.

"How do you know?"

"They diagnosed it, even then. Pregnancy and childbirth were very dangerous for her. So was life at high altitudes, stress, and hard work."

*The thin woman is sitting in the sand beside a wide river. In the far distance a bridge spans the water. At her feet two children are poking twigs into a sand castle. Two tents have been pitched under a tree on her right. An iron kettle hangs over a fire. Hatless, the woman has scraped her hair straight back into a small bun. Her blouse and skirt are extremely plain. Not noticing either the children or the photographer, she stares across the river and into a distance beyond camera range.*

"Camping along the Colorado," explained Lynn.

"No more parasol," said Catherine, examining the picture closely. "Her skin is still smoother than mine. But maybe she does look ill."

*13 June 1902*

*Cooked fish. George is building a boat. Children both very sunburnt.*

*15 June*

*Terribly hot. Today Baby tumbled into the river but his skirts floated him downstream, and Sissy pulled him out. Thank God. Palpitations.*

There was also a packet of letters with English stamps, addressed to Mrs. George Standish, Flagstaff, Arizona Territory.

*2 November 1903*

*Dear Lavinia,*

*We thought of you at the Royal College of Music concert. Mr. Coleridge Taylor played some of his violin compositions, and Cecilia accompanied him on the piano. Papa and I were proud of her. Do you still find time for your music, my dear?*

"In 1905 the doctor ordered a change of scene," continued Lynn. "So they moved to San Diego. The sea air was supposed to be good for invalids."

*The porch is encircled by a white railing. Each of the three women occupies a rocking chair; the three men lean against the railing. Everyone gazes straight ahead, except for George, who is looking anxiously at Lavinia, and Lavinia, who is looking away.*

"I don't know who the other people in that picture are," Lynn said.

"I can see the ocean in the background," said Catherine. "You know, she looks like Mother."

"Mother's much older now than Lavinia ever was."

*9 Aug. '07*

*Bad night. George took the children to bathe. I stayed upstairs all day. Feet swollen. Doctor came.*

10 *Aug.*

*Better again. George carried me down to the parlour. Sissy has learned to dive. Coughed at night.*

*15 Aug.*

*George wishes to hire a nurse. If only I could breathe better. Children very good. Doctor.*

*21 Aug.*

*Someone playing the piano down the street. Very tired.*

"Her diary ends there," Lynn said.

"But there are more entries."

Lynn shook her head. "That's George's handwriting."

*23 Aug.*

*Better night. Children up to visit. Doctor.*

*24 Aug.*

*Sleepless night.*

*25 Aug. 1907*

*By midday she said there was no light and air in our room. I carried her down to a bed in the garden and brought the children to say good-bye. At half past three I lost the best little wife a man could ever have.*

*Good-bye, sweetheart. I feel nothing but pain.*

"And look at this," Lynn said hastily, over the lump in her throat. "It was stuck in the diary—a prescription for the last day of her life."

"Whiskey!"

"It was all they could do for her."

"Oh, Lynnie!"

Turning her face away, Lynn dragged a black iron box as big as a footstool from beneath her desk. At a distance, her children were fighting. Shrieks were followed by thumps, then loud weeping. She heard her husband's deep voice and wondered if she should intervene, but silence fell without her.

"Every year, on the anniversary of her death, George wrote Lavinia a letter and put it away in this strongbox. Nobody's ever opened them."

Catherine clapped her hands. "Let's do it!"

Lynn shook her head doubtfully, lifting the heavy lid. The sealed envelopes gleamed up at her.

"Lynn, it's a treasure. What a book it would make! And all the research is done."

"Well—" She felt her ears grow hot.

"I have some contacts."

Lynn said nothing.

"And I can write."

Lynn slammed the lid shut, and her anger boiled over.

"You! It's all *you*. These are real people's lives, not transcendental meditation or Latin American politics."

"Of course," said Catherine, puzzled.

Her color had risen, Lynn saw; that used to be a sign of temper. It was strange how even after twenty years she knew the meaning of her sister's smallest mannerisms. That bright mocking smile: she was angry.

"I would just edit—"

"No. You won't take this away. Where were you when the work got done? Where were you when Daddy died?"

"Lynnie, I'm sorry—"

"It's too late."

"I hope it's not," said Catherine. Now she was using charm, Lynn thought. "Didn't Mother tell you? I'm going to live here again. I think it's time for a change."

Lynn retorted that people never changed. Catherine said that Lavinia had: from English spinster to pioneer wife and mother.

"Yes, and it killed her."

"Lynn, *you* need a change. Do the book. Travel."

"I can't."

Lynn clutched the strongbox. Her head churned. She remembered her husband and children, her house, the piles of dingy books at work, all the annoying borrowers with problems. There were too many books in the world already, she thought.

Catherine took her hand and squeezed it.

*25 August 1908*

*My dear little sweetheart,*

*It has been a hard and sad year since you left us. I remember you many times every day. I am much the same; hair a trifle thinner, perhaps. I do my best with the children, but I fear I'm rather gruff and rough with them, compared to you. We have returned to Arizona, where I am building us a house. I would give all I have (including the children, though you would never agree) to see you walk through the door, or to hear you sing again. Sissy's voice gives me a chill sometimes. Good-bye, sweetheart, until next year, at least. I find some comfort in writing this, as I do in looking at your things. I truly cannot say that I believe we'll meet again, but you will always be a part of us, my love.*

*George*

The sisters put their arms around each other and wept.

"He outlived her by forty years," Lynn said. "Do you know what else he kept in that box? Her ashes."

"Where are they now?"

"In the end they were buried together."

"Ah!"

"He married again, of course. But that's another story."

Standing on her father's lawn, young Lavinia watched them soberly. Lynn shivered, unable to meet her gaze for long. The iron box yawned at their feet.

"He killed her," Lynn said. She felt as flat as a photograph, dim and dry.

A neighbor's Christmas lights blinked inanely through the dark. A dripping faucet, Lynn thought; a tolling bell.

"No," said Catherine in triumph. "He loved her. And look—we're here. Aren't we?"

# Childish Things

To toughen him up, the men thrust five-year-old Gordon McPherson into the saddle behind Loco Manuel, the cowboy, and carried him along on roundups. All day Gordon would bang against Loco Manuel's hard spine, elbows, and .45. The boy's knees and buttocks ached. At night he cried himself to sleep, sucking his thumb and clutching a ragged doll.

His mother had made it for him when he was a baby; nowadays he tried to keep it hidden.

The Depression hung over their small cattle ranch. They were dirt-poor, his father said, putting a bitter spin on the words. But they weren't as poor as the tribe of Okies who had camped in the yard one night, crossing southern Arizona on their way to California. In the morning Gordon saw that they all wore clothes made of flour sacks.

"They must live on biscuits," his mother said in awe when they were gone.

Gordon couldn't remember better times. Today he gripped the saddle, not wanting to put his arms around Loco Manuel.

"*Niñita. . . .*" whispered Loco Manuel.

"I'm not a girl."

"Where's your doll, eh?"

Gordon stiffened. Who had told him? The three horses plodded single file through the cactus and mesquite brush. By leaning sideways Gordon could see his father's high, narrow shoulders bobbing in rhythm with his horse. Not Dad, he thought. Dad didn't hold conversations with Loco Manuel; he just told him what to do. Was it Bud, Gordon's older brother? He looked at Bud's back, a thinner copy of Dad's. But Bud was nice to him, mostly.

In spite of the eleven years between them, the boys sometimes banded together against their sister Alice. She was not allowed to skip school for a roundup, or to hunt mountain lions. Early that morning, which now seemed very long ago to Gordon, their mother had laid down the law.

"At least one of my children is going to get an education," she said. She stretched her long hank of hair out straight from her scalp, twisted it into a knot, and began to pierce it with gray hairpins.

Behind her back Alice squeezed out a nasty scowl at her brothers.

Alice was twelve. She liked to haunt the corrals and the barn; she could stick tight on the spookiest horses. Alice must have betrayed him.

By the time they reached the Sopilote pasture, where they were rounding up that day, the white sun stood halfway up the sky. The riders fanned out across the rocky foothills to look for cows and their calves. In this dry country, at least forty acres were needed to support each animal. Roundups were hard.

"Hoosh! Hoosh!" shouted Dad and Bud as they herded.

"Hoosh!" shouted Loco Manuel, with less conviction.

Gordon rode where he did because Loco Manuel was the clumsiest cowboy of the three. Bud had surpassed him some time ago. Loco Manuel's head was a bit too small for his body, and even his Spanish sounded funny to Gordon. He had a way of dropping a rope at the wrong moment and starting to sing. But he did know how to ride. He liked to talk to the horses, though sometimes he was also cruel to them.

"He's the best cowboy we can afford," Gordon's father used to say.

Like the cattle, Loco Manuel could live on very little.

The May morning was almost as hot as July. Soon the white-faced cattle were panting, the calves stumbling. The men penned them up against a cliff, then squatted in the tatters of shade beneath a mesquite and ate lunch. Tongues hanging out, the cows watched them.

"Indians used this canyon as a route across the Mexican border," Gordon's father said.

In places the rock walls looked like masonry. Lines of trees and bushes marked the watercourses, but only one full stock tank glinted, five miles away.

Gordon thought of the two-room school at the mouth of the canyon where his mother taught the younger class. She was reading them a story called *The Water Babies*, about a dirty little chimney sweep named Tom, who fell into a stream and was transformed. Gordon would miss today's chapter.

"Once," said his father, "when I was about Gordon's age, I went out to the barn alone and found it full of Yaqui Indians, on the run from the Mexican army."

"What did you do?" asked Bud.

"Shut the door again!"

Gordon sucked on the canteen. Earlier that year he and Bud had come upon a long canvas bundle in the barn. Gordon wasn't supposed to know, but he had overheard, that it was a dead body. A Border Patrolman had been shot in the mountains. Their mother made Gordon and Alice stay indoors until the bundle was taken away.

In the afternoon they drove the cattle across a mesa. It was hot work but easier than going down the canyon. A pair of black buzzards kept pace with them, effortlessly riding the air.

"*Amor, amorcito de mi vida*," hummed Loco Manuel. "How's it going, pretty little girl?"

"Shut your mouth."

Loco Manuel laughed.

They reached the edge of the mesa. The ranch headquarters lay directly below them at the base of a steep slope. Craning his neck, Gordon saw the wooden corrals, the windmill, the barn, the old stone house, and the two dark green flames of the cypress trees on either side. His mother's pomegranate bush was in bloom. Relief washed over him.

The cattle bawled and bellowed, stamping their feet and rolling their large eyes rimmed with white fur lashes.

"Hoosh!" cried Gordon's father, and he and Bud pushed the herd toward the trail, which dropped in switchbacks to the canyon bottom. But instead of following them, Loco Manuel let out a series of falsetto yips and dug his spurs into his horse.

"*Ay-y-y-y!*" he howled, plunging straight downhill.

The horse panicked, boulders thudded behind them, and mesquite thorns bloodied Gordon's face. The hooves struck sparks from the rocks. Gordon closed his eyes. He clung to Loco Manuel all the way down, hating him.

Dad lifted him off at the bottom.

"I ain't cryin'," Gordon said.

"Good." His father turned to Loco Manuel and said in the deadly quiet voice that was worse than his rages: "You will not do that again."

Halfway to the house the lion hounds met him, lifting their muzzles in song and swatting him with their heavy tails. Gordon trudged on. His legs were no longer wobbly, just stiff. The grains of dust felt large on his tongue, and he could also taste a little blood.

When he reached the house he put his face to the screen door and listened. From behind him came the protests of the cattle being driven into the corral, and the wordless shouts of the men. Inside the house it was dim and quiet, except for an occasional clink from the kitchen, where Mother and Alice must be cooking supper. Then he heard their voices.

"Catastrophe," said his mother.

"C-a-t-a-s-t-r-o-p-h-e," Alice answered.

"Good. Indomitable."

They were practicing Alice's spelling list. Gordon slipped through the screen door and tiptoed to the bedroom that he shared with Bud. As silently as possible, he hunted through the top dresser drawer for his brother's .22 pistol. Bud shot jackrabbits with it, which Mother made into stew, and he had showed Gordon how to load and fire the pistol. Gordon fumbled with the slippery cartridges at first but finally made them fit into the cylinder.

"M-e-t-a," spelled Alice, "m-o-r-p-h—"

Gordon closed the door gently behind himself.

A black mark blossomed between the eyes of the figure leaning against the hackberry tree. Before anyone found him, Gordon dug a hole and buried his doll.

# Los Mojados

From behind the San Ysidro Mountains, clouds rose and swelled into the shape of anvils.

The windbells set up a clamor. This brought two people out on the porch, the old man probing his way with two canes, followed by his daughter-in-law.

"Rain coming?" She had been roasting green chiles, and the smell of burnt pepper hovered around her.

"Well, Linda," he said, intent on something, "I'd be surprised."

He usually loved to pass on his lore, so she waited.

"They're pretty dark," she observed at last.

"You want 'em dark and low," Joe McPherson said. "Touching the mountains. Those are flying too high."

Under the hackberry tree two hounds, Beauty and Beast, lay with heads lifted and soft ears dangling. The jumbled music of the windbells died away. In its place Joe and Linda heard first nothing, then the friction of leaf against leaf, the creak of the windmill, and the rush of water in the canyon down below. But it was only the runoff from a summer storm and would soon dry up. "Well," she said, drifting toward the door, "we sure could use some rain."

"We could always use it."

Linda opened the screen door for him, but he hesitated.

"No. I'll stay here for a while." Letting his bulk drop into a lawn chair, he added angrily: "I'm no good for anything now."

"Oh, Dad." Linda put one arm around him and gave him an awkward hug. Jutting from his cool inert flesh, the shoulder bones were surprisingly sharp. "That's not true."

He snorted but seemed slightly pleased. Linda remembered her fear when Bud had first brought her to the ranch as a lanky city girl of nineteen. Joe McPherson had been formidable in his prime. Everything changed on the day they brought him down from the mountains with two crushed legs. His temper was better now, and Mrs. McPherson was dead.

The kitchen was all Linda's. Sometimes she wondered if her mother-in-law had simply quit rather than nurse Joe—if the accident had killed *her*—and then Linda would feel half sorry. Many real troubles had turned Mrs. McPherson sour and tedious: that was her worst misfortune. And actually the family managed pretty well together in the main ranch house, with the cowboy in the small house where Bud and Linda had spent their first ten years. Their son was a grown man now, and their daughter was a college sophomore up in Tucson. Lanky no longer, Linda had become a capable ranch wife. As she pulled a pan of smoking chiles from the broiler, she nearly giggled out loud, thinking of what Mrs. McPherson would have said to see her wrap them in newspaper to cool, just like a Mexican.

"You peel the skin off anyway, so what does it matter?" she thought.

Joe McPherson lit a cigarette. The smoke went straight up, he noticed, and the damn fool windbells were quiet. Sometimes they kept him awake at night. But Linda was a good kid, didn't fuss much. Hell of a thing to get old, he often thought. Ninety years old! "I never wanted no ninety years," he said to himself, surveying his legs and his canes with contempt.

Still, gazing up at the clouds as they mounted over the peaks, he felt contentment fill him like a liquid with only a trace of bitterness in it. He clearly recalled seeing Apache campfires at dusk high up in the San Ysidros. Then his father used to call the children in for the night, as he remembered Indian massacres. Geronimo had ridden through this country: Arizona Territory, they called it till 1912. Joe's gaze traveled down the mountains to the lower slopes, where the dusty purple was scarred by a series of pale road cuts. They were the remains of a land fraud, a subdivision never built.

"Sidewinder tracks," thought Joe McPherson, shifting uncomfortably in his chair.

He had leveled a double-barreled shotgun at the land speculator. Then Joe took a grim delight in having charges pressed against him; he put on a fine show with the canes in court. Since the speculator was a stranger in Santa Gertrudis County and had trespassed upon the McPherson porch, Joe got off with a lecture. It was not the first time he'd pulled a gun on someone, or fired it, to tell the truth. But no one seemed to remember the range wars of seventy years ago anymore.

A burst of song tumbled down the hill from the cowboy's house: "*Porque somos los mojados, siempre nos busca la ley. . . .*" Reynaldo was playing the radio while he worked on his old pickup truck. Joe grunted to himself. Personally he preferred Western music. Yet as he listened to the words of this song, a sly little smile turned up the corners of mustache. It was a *corrido*, a country ballad with a brisk beat.

> Because we are wetbacks
> The law is always after us,
> For we are illegal
> And we don't speak English . . . .
> Our problem is easy to solve
> If we find a *gringuita* to marry!

For the second time that afternoon Joe sensed a disturbance in the air. It was neither the song nor the wind.

> When the wetback goes on strike . . . .
> Onion . . . lettuce . . . lemon . . . all rot.
> All the dance halls close. . . .

Impudent horns, sad strings. Joe leaned forward, cursing the music and his failing senses.

> *¡Vivan todos los mojados!*
> Immigrants, vacationers,
> And the ones who plan to get married
> To solve their problems.

The hounds jumped up and ran baying across the yard: a small man had appeared at the edge of the clearing. His thin brownish clothes clung to his body as garments do when they are much worn and slept in. He looked up at the ranch house. Then he began sidestepping as Beauty and Beast reached him.

To Linda's surprise Joe was standing upright without the canes, calling off the dogs.

"Why, Dad—"

"Wetbacks," he said. A second figure now stood behind the first. The pack of hounds and miscellaneous dogs drew back grudgingly.

"*Oye*," Joe called. "*Vénganse acá*."

The figures obeyed, moving slowly toward the house. They hunched their shoulders humbly but stared all around with a certain bravado.

"Where's Buddy?"

"Up on the mesa," Linda said, "fixing that pump."

Joe clutched at the porch railing.

"Hadn't you better sit down, Dad?"

He ignored her. "Who are you? What do you want?" he demanded in his guttural Spanish.

The two men standing at the foot of the steps rattled off their names. They had come from the south, Jalisco and Nayarit, they said; they were looking for work.

"Not much here," said Joe.

They had friends in Phoenix, they answered.

"That's a long way. More than two hundred miles," Joe told them.

"Do you have water?" blurted Linda.

They seemed to be completely empty handed. But in a moment the younger and handsomer of the pair said that they had left their water with a companion up the hill.

"How many of you are there?" barked Joe.

Gradually four others appeared, ducking through the mequite trees that bordered the canyon like green tangles of wire.

"Can't we do something here?" asked the handsome Mexican. The others waited in the yard, kicking the dust, while he mounted first one step and then another. Joe shook his head impatiently and spoke English sideways to Linda.

"When's Buddy coming back?"

"I don't know. He missed lunch. But he knows there are riders coming at five."

"Okay." With a spurt of his old vigor Joe took two or three steps forward. "We'll give you all two hours' work around the yard. For food."

"Only food?"

"Who knows? Let's see how you work." He looked over his shoulder "Linda, tell them what to do in the garden."

They watched the men scatter until the scene was nearly back to normal, except for the figures bowed over their work. The radio had stopped playing.

Linda hadn't seen him walk alone in years. She knew he did not want the wetbacks to think he was old and crippled and she was unprotected. This idea flustered her curiously; she felt desirable for a moment, like a heroine of the paperback romances that she furtively read.

Her thoughts skittered about: "Sandwiches, canned fruit. Reynaldo's here, too. No need to worry. But would he—? No. Still, he'll tell them the truth perhaps. So was it all a show? For nothing? Machismo . . . ."

Surely, she thought, Bud would come home any minute now, hungry too. She decided to hard-boil some eggs. Why should she be scared of some poor souls crossing the desert at the peak of summer, with almost nothing in the world but the clothes on their backs?

Linda filled several plastic bottles with clean water. She kept a supply of old containers for this purpose because more illegal aliens had flowed through the ranch lately than ever before. From the Mexican border they followed the El Paso Natural Gas pipeline through the mountains. Bud used to hire them for odd jobs, to build a wall or string a fence, but recently the McPhersons had felt too poor to pay more than Reynaldo's salary. Their cattle allotment had been cut, the price of beef was down, and everything else was up: they had stretched almost as far as they could. Linda wondered what her husband would think about this crew of workers today, but after all it was still Joe McPherson's ranch.

One of the wetbacks came into view through the kitchen window, a middle-aged man with a broad Indian face, round head, and streaks of gray in his hair. "About my age," Linda thought, watching him draw a rake through the dirt in the side yard. She could also hear the thump of a hoe against the weeds in the back.

"Where will they all end up?" Linda asked herself.

It was a game, a cross between hide-and-seek and a manhunt. The immigration officials and the Border Patrol—*la Migra*, the wetbacks called them, or *los verdes*—were pitted against the "illegals," the "wets," translated *mojados*. But there was no river to cross into Arizona, only a fence in places.

Joe sat caressing the living leather of Beauty's ear.

"Pain tonight," he reminded himself, though excitement still warmed his blood. In some ways he liked pain, which was almost all he had left to fight. Not that he was a quiet stoic. He was rude to doctors and especially to nurses; he drank too much bourbon and refused his medicine; he swore and complained. But late at night he and the pain would face each other and he would hold his territory. Sometimes he could even force it away by riding in his mind along one of the trails that crossed his ranch.

He'd always liked horses seventeen or eighteen hands high. As he rode through the nights he could feel in his bones the places where the barbed mesquites made you duck. It was a harsh, hard-baked country; Joe loved it with a passionate awe that he had never felt for a human being. The image of his dissatisfied wife had faded, but he could recall exactly how a trickle of water had slipped between two boulders daubed with green and yellow lichen, in 1922. "My land," he would whisper to himself on a hilltop. "My place."

Although the McPhersons had begun to buy old Jeeps after World War II, they still needed horses to penetrate the roadless mountains. They kept a pack of hounds—out of habit, and because Joe liked hounds, and also because sometimes a mountain lion would start killing calves. Joe used to say that lion hunts were work, not sport, yet he knew in his heart that his happiest times were those wild final chases after the singing hounds. More often than not, the lion escaped. At no other time did Joe allow his horses to be run. He scoffed at the riding in Western movies, and at the unreality. "Candyboxes," he called them. However, Linda found him more and more often hunched over the television set, watching John Wayne or Gary Cooper or even Clint Eastwood, with the volume turned up to a roar.

"For Buddy now," Joe reflected, flipping a match to the ground, "it really is work."

Reynaldo came strolling across the yard and greeted the newcomers. He was a good cowboy, the kind you could hardly find among Anglos anymore, let alone afford to hire. He had worked for the McPhersons ever since Joe's accident; certainly he was loyal and dependable, as far as any man in his position could be. Reynaldo was a wetback, too, of course. Wearing tight new Levi's and an old Western shirt that had once belonged to Joe, he came up to the porch.

"My ghost!" the old man thought wryly.

"Where's *el Buddy?*"

Joe bristled somewhat. "Coming down from the mesa. Why?"

Reinaldo shrugged. "Maybe he's got more work for those guys."

"Have you fed the heifers yet?"

"I'm going right now."

On impulse Linda carried one of the jugs outside and offered water to the man with the rake. As he drank, the boy who had been hoeing came shyly up, and when she put a cup in his hand a pang of memory ran through her. How long had it been since she fed her own son?

"Where are you from?" she asked.

The boy pronounced a long name that meant nothing to her. Seeing this he drew a postcard from his pocket: the main plaza of a small town in the jungle, trees weighted down with flame-colored flowers.

"*Muy bonito,*" Linda said, touched.

The older man now brought out a lump of rock and broke into a long speech. Look, he said, it was gold. He'd found it as they hiked, he knew precisely where, and there was more, much more. He would return and mine it after he sold this nugget in Phoenix.

Linda looked doubtfully at the greenish, faceted mineral lying in the palm of a hand so thickened by labor that it looked like a foot.

"I don't know. It's metal," she volunteered.

"Gold," said the man and returned it to his pocket.

"*Ándale*," said a low voice behind them. It was the good-looking leader. Linda was started to find him suddenly so close; she saw the individual blue-black hairs in his heavy mustache, then the eyes, shaded by a straw cowboy hat with a sweat stain all around the band. "Come on," he said. "After we finish we still have to find a place to sleep."

From that point on, the man with the rake worked erratically. After a while he wandered around to the front of the house, talking to himself.

At four o'clock the Jeep jerked into the yard, backfiring and threatening to die all the way to the barn, and when Bud stamped up the steps he was as furious as possible for someone with his easygoing temperament. Linda was disturbed to see him slam his hat onto the rack.

"I should've shoved that goddamned Jeep off the cliff in the Tecolote pasture. I've been tinkering with it since noon."

"What's wrong with it?" asked Joe, with his little smile.

"Fuel line, I think."

Linda brought iced tea.

"I need a *drink*," Bud said.

Joe helped himself to the bourbon too. Linda leaned in the doorway.

"Who's that outside? More wetbacks?"

"Would you like a sandwich, honey?"

"I told 'em to work two hours for food," Joe said. "Place was full of weeds," he added, a touch of belligerence coloring his tone.

"The kids used to help in the garden," Linda said, defensive in turn.

"Never mind." Bud's flushed face had returned to normal, and he sat back in his chair. "I sure could eat something, Linda. I could eat that damn Jeep."

Spreading margarine, she raised her head. Surely she heard the sound of a car approaching? But it was too early, still too hot for the paying horseback riders who came out from town looking for a taste of the old West.

"*¡La Migra!*" shouted Reynaldo.

The three McPhersons went to the living room window. A pale green and cream colored pickup truck was fording the canyon.

"Well," said Bud calmly, "they're on their own."

"What do you mean? What'll you say?" Linda felt a cold flutter in her chest.

"No need to say anything," said Joe.

The truck succeeded in crossing the canyon. Herded by baying dogs, it climbed the dusty hill to the house. Outside, silence had fallen, and not a single straw hat was visible. Linda hoped that nothing would happen; in the face of trouble and suffering she always wanted to shrink into something insignificant, a dry leaf or a mark on the wall. She wasn't lazy; she carried her load. Year after year, however, each time a truckload of cattle went off to market she closed herself in her bedroom and wept.

"You know, I heard something about wetbacks on the radio, coming down from the mesa."

"What?"

"I don't know, Dad. Didn't hear the whole thing."

"Government!" Joe spat out the word. "Nobody used to care who was born on what side of the Line. I say, if they want to work, let 'em."

Two men wearing different uniforms, one crisp green and the other wrinkled khaki, got out of the truck and fended off the dogs.

"That's Rubén Salinas," Bud said.

"You weren't here today, Buddy," Joe urged. "You don't know anything about it." Deep in their leathery sockets his eyeballs gleamed, whites bloodshot, pupils speckled with gold.

"He's a sheriff's deputy, Dad, not *la Migra*."

Linda jumped when the knock sounded at the door.

"You folks sure live a long way out," said the officer in green, pressing close to the screen door.

"Hey, Buddy," said the sheriff's deputy.

"How you doing, Rubén."

The gloomy room was full of hunting trophies and old-fashioned furniture. The old man was sunk in a heavy brown armchair, one cane propped on either side; Linda was poised in the doorway to the dining room.

Rubén said, "Seen any wetbacks lately?"

"Why?" snapped Joe.

The two officers' heads wheeled in his direction.

Bud rubbed his corrugated forehead slowly, and Linda saw that he had reached a decision. "Yeah, there were some men here just now."

The heads turned back. "How many?"

"I don't know. My wife and my dad here talked to them."

Joe, gnawing on his chagrin, imagined how he would escape if he were one of them. *Sálvase quien pueda*: save yourself whoever can. Alone. Get out of sight first. Into the mesquite thickets and over the hill, quietly. That might be a four-wheel-drive pickup outside, but they had no horses, no dogs. Escape was simple, really. Lay low for a while, then reconnoiter. Night coming. Half moon. Good for walking. Back in Mexico by morning.

"This is serious," Rubén said. "I may as well tell you there's been a murder."

That morning a rancher over at Piedras Blancas, ten miles north, had been found shot to death in his truck. There were footprints running into the mountains, and a witness had seen the rancher yesterday with a group of wetbacks.

"All available law enforcement personnel have been called onto the case," said the Border Patrolman. His little mustache was trimmed into the shape of an eyebrow. Joe stared at him offensively, but after a glance he turned away.

"Ignoring the old cripple," Joe thought.

"We're notifying isolated ranches," the *verde* continued, "and looking for the trail."

"You'd have better luck on a horse," said Joe.

"We have an infrared device that senses body heat," the young man said.

"Right now we have a murder," interrupted Rubén. "In my jurisdiction."

Joe could picture the hunt even better than the escape: horses laboring up the hills, hounds scattering in liquid motion, gun in his hand. It would be pitifully easy on a day like this. Still, a man, however clumsy and thirsty, might be cannier than a mountain lion, and maybe some of these men were murderers, and armed. He revolved that idea in his mind.

Seventy years ago, Joe and his father were running cattle all the way from the mountains to the Kino River. They caused trouble by fencing formerly open range, and McPherson fences collapsed mysteriously, while McPherson cows vanished overnight. One evening Joe and his father rode down the canyon to check on a herd grazing in the meadows along the Kino, which ran all year round in those days. It was calving season.

When they rounded the last hill before the river, they came upon a scene that never lost its power over Joe. Even now, brooding in his armchair, he could call up a burst of pure rage. He saw a group of men from nearby ranches. They had cut the fence and driven two or three dozen head of their own cows through the gap to graze and drink. Now the men were standing in a circle, passing a bottle around. For light, and out of sheer devilry they had set a number of cholla cactus plants on fire.

Joe galloped ahead of his father, feeling like a hot steel spear. Yelling, he flung himself off the horse and reached for the nearest man's neck; he happened to choose a cowboy named Enrique Macías, who worked for the Sperrys to the south. Macías raised a hand, and Joe saw the knife edge flicker. Afterward he remembered his father's shout and the orange flare in the dark but not the shot itself. Macías sat down in the grass and died before the cactus was entirely burnt out.

The knife helped to save Joe, but not nearly as much as the fact that Macías was a Mexican. Self defense, the jury decided, and after a while every rancher in the county built fences. For years Joe's name raised eyebrows, but gradually the scandal faded away. He had to pass the site of the shooting every time he left the ranch or worked in the river pasture. At first Enrique Macías seemed always to be there, curled in the grass with his knife. As the decades went by and the river dried up, except during summer floods, Macías disappeared too. He visited Joe McPherson during a fever, in an occasional dream, and in moments of glorious fury and fear. After the land speculator had stumbled down the porch steps, Macías faced Joe from the bottom.

"You can't stop it," he said. "*Verás. Tu tiempo vendrá.*"

You'll see. Your time will come.

Joe tightened his grip on his cane.

"There were six of them," Linda was saying in a nearly inaudible voice. "All different ages."

"I told 'em they could work for some food," Joe cut in.

"Are you aware, sir," said *la Migra*, "of the legalities of the situation?"

"How'm I supposed to know who's legal?"

"Let's get on with this," Rubén said irritably. He appeared to have sweated profusely earlier in the day. "Can you give us a description?"

The leader wore a mustache and a cowboy hat, Linda recalled. Joe said flatly that they looked like out-of-work Mexicans. Rubén asked if the McPhersons had noticed any bloodstains. No? How about the men's shoes?

"Did any of them wear track shoes?" asked the other officer eagerly.

Rubén glared at him, but just then spasmodic static burst from the walkie-talkie on his belt. Although the message was gibberish to the McPhersons, it brought both visitors to their feet.

"We got to go," Rubén said abruptly. "They think they spotted 'em over at the Onslow place. Don't take any more risks, folks. Call if you see anything, eh?"

The sound of the motor trailed away.

"Footprints all over the yard," remarked Joe.

Bud gave his father a look. "Did you see those track shoes?"

"Nah."

"Linda?"

She shook her head. Track shoes sounded like a young person, she thought. What did that boy have on his feet? Nobody could walk four or five miles to the Onslow place in fifteen minutes. But when was the last time she had seen them?

A cloud structure now filled the eastern third of the sky. Great bulges pressed upward like a clump of clenched fists. The late afternoon sunlight fell slanting over the dust, exaggerating the prints of dogs' paws, street shoes, work boots, cowboy boots, and sandals.

"Well," said Bud, "I didn't really think so."

He and Linda stood by the vegetable garden, now half weeded, and watched the first signs of evening appear. Flights of birds crossed the canyon; stinging gnats began to dim the air. The worst weight of the heat was lifting. The windmill groaned a little, the chimes jingled, and somewhere in the distance a low hum started.

"What's that?" cried Linda. "A car? It must be the riders."

"Hell. I forgot."

"Maybe you shouldn't ride today."

"Scare 'em off? But it's an easy fifty dollars." Bud resettled his hat upon his head and started for the corral. "Nothing's going to happen," he said.

The dudes, as Joe liked to call them, scrambled out of their shiny sedan and waited in the manure. They were dressed in pastel clothing first invented for the sports of the British leisure class. Embarrassed, Linda quickly went back to the house.

Her father-in-law was sitting in his favorite armchair with a shotgun across his lap.

"How about a game of cribbage?" he asked gravely.

"Not with that."

"It needed cleaning," Joe said.

"Now, Dad—" He was shameless. The pungent smell of gun cleaner hung in the air; Linda stooped automatically and gathered up a dirty swab from the flowered carpet. Joe lifted the gun and sighted down the barrels, taking aim at the head of a mountain lion that he had shot twenty years before. After his accident he'd given Bud his hunting rifle.

First the lion killed five calves, he remembered. Then it led him on a tremendous chase. After his kill he followed the pack horse carrying the lion's skin down to the ranch, and for five hours he was struck again and again with the beauty of the pelt. Seven feet long, it shaded gradually in color from tawny along the spine to rough gray over the belly: exactly the same colors as the crags where the animal, a young tom, had died. Joe got off his horse in a black mood that drove everyone away for days. He stayed in his armchair in the living room, one hand wrapped around a glass, staring out of the window, itching for a fight, until the liquor was gone and the cloud lifted. The taxidermy cost more than they really could afford.

"Please put that thing down," Linda said, and he set the gun aside.

She brought the board, the cards, and a small table. Dinner was already cooked. The tide of larger events moved on in spite of the two of them. There was nothing to do but wait, and at such times cribbage was a tradition of theirs. They were quite evenly matched in the game, for although he was shameless, she was methodical.

Presently Joe said: "No track shoes, eh?"

"No. But I wondered—did you see the one with the gold nugget?"

"Fool's gold."

"It's terrible about that rancher."

Joe grunted.

As the second game began, someone rapped at the door. Linda gasped and let her cards go fluttering into her lap.

"Probably Reynaldo," said Joe levelly. "Go see."

Linda forced herself to look and was not surprised to see the leader of the *mojados* banging on the door.

"*¡Ábrame la puerta, señora!*"

"Go ahead," ordered the old man. "Open it."

Linda pushed her hair out of her eyes and thought wildly of running away, of a dreamlike, cartoonlike escape. She turned the doorknob and faced the handsome Mexican, who was alone. Reflected in his brown eyes she saw her tiny self; she imagined his fingertips on her throat, her body thrown across a horse.

"*Señora*, we worked; now give us our food."

"*Muy bien*," called Joe from behind her. " '*Pérate un momento*. Go pack it up, Linda."

When she returned with bags and water jugs, everything in the living room was still except for Joe's thick misshapen fingers, toying with the shotgun. Handing over the supplies, Linda noticed the young man's rank odor and the fresh red scratches on his hands and face.

"Stay away from the natural gas pipeline," said Joe suddenly. "They patrol it. And they're looking for some wetbacks who killed a rancher."

Linda held her breath. The Mexican, who had been peering into the bags, raised his head and confronted Joe and Linda blankly.

"*¿Ah, sí?*" he said, but that was all. He paused and, as coolly as a shopper, asked Linda for one more thing.

"Soap?" she said.

"Why not?" growled Joe.

Linda watched the young man's straight back in its thin brown shirt, its muscles slightly knotted under its burden, until the figure disappeared up the canyon.

When she turned around, Joe said: "We'll have to start the game over. I saw your cards."

"Dad—"

"Did I ever tell you," he interrupted, "about the time the rattlesnake crawled over my face?"

He shuffled the cards stiffly.

"No, I don't think you did," Linda answered.

"Well, I was working in the mountains. Lost a bull up there—oh, maybe forty years ago. Hobbled the horse and slept in a cave. It was winter. The snake woke me in the middle of the night. I knew what it was; I could hear the rattles. Besides, a snake smells. Small snake, probably young. And I just laid there and let it crawl. Seemed like a lifetime. Finally it went slithering down my head and away and I sat up and lit a candle. Sure enough, there he was, with his little beady eyes. I looked at him, and I said, 'All right, I won't strike you either.' And in the morning he was gone."

Linda let out a long sigh. "You've had a lot of close calls, Dad."

"Too many." The old man held out the pack for her to cut. "I should've died up in the mountains. Bleached along with the cow bones."

"No, Dad."

He looked at her oddly. "Cut," he said, and she did. "Should've tanned my hide and hung it with the others," he went on, with perverse humor. "Or given me to a museum. Soon you can."

"Dad!"

"Stop it now, stop it," he said. "*Así es la vida.* Go ahead. Play. It's your turn."

Later, as she leaned over the stove, Linda heard more tears dropping upon the hot metal with faint hisses. All her life she had worked, served, cleaned, patched, and preserved in the hope of somehow reaching . . . what? Rest? Peace? She had an idea of happiness—merely a time when nothing pained her. As she aged she began to realize when that time would probably come.

Bud came home at sunset, simmering with suppressed laughter. Linda could see that he was saving the joke for the supper table, and as soon as the three of them sat down, he tilted back his chair and broke into chuckles.

"Those darn wetbacks!" he said. "You know the pool in the rocks at the old homestead? Well, I brought the riders around that bend today and one of the gals let out a scream. There were your wetbacks, naked as jaybirds, splashing away."

"So that's why he wanted soap," Linda said guiltily.

Bud stopped laughing. "They came back while I was gone?"

"Just one," said Joe. "I figured we owed 'em something."

"Owed 'em what? Why's the shotgun in the living room?"

Joe's mustache twitched rhythmically as he chewed. Linda glanced from one man to the other, then down at the tablecloth; she knew these struggles by heart.

This time, as usual, her husband shrugged. "Well," he drawled, "I'm too tired to dig a grave tonight."

The corners of the mustache turned up, and Joe reached for the salt. During dessert Bud asked if they had seen Reynaldo yet; Linda shook her head.

"I've got a notion he's hiding in the Indian cave," Joe said.

"Maybe *la Migra* will start to pester us now," Bud said.

"If they take him," said Joe, "he'll just walk across the Line the next day."

"Maybe so."

After dinner they watched the ten o'clock news, which was full of the murder at Piedras Blancas. Drug smuggling and robbery were mentioned. Two suspects were being held without bail at the Santa Gertrudis County Jail and others were supposed to be at large. "Chances of thunderstorms—" began the grinning weather man, but Bud snuffed him out in the middle of a word. Without the aqua light of television the objects in the living room looked humdrum and solid, except for the ghostly animals mounted high up on the walls.

"I wonder if that dude ever looked at the sky," muttered Joe.

"As much as anybody, I guess," said Bud. "Want a hand to bed, Dad?"

The old man persisted. "Now, that movie they made about Geronimo. Showed him in a pool hall. Pure trash. My father knew a man who helped catch Geronimo."

"He massacred those people up the canyon," Linda put in. Although she hated the bloody details of that story, somehow the words slipped out. She hoped Joe wouldn't tell it again.

"This man," said Joe, "Asa Walker was his name. He saw Geronimo once years afterward, when they'd put him in a Wild West show. Walker used to call him 'old Geronimee.' He used to say—" and the old man narrowed his eyes, mimicking another old man's boast, " 'and I saw *him*, and he saw *me* . . . old Geronimee.' "

His laugh turned into a cough.

"Took him off to Oklahoma, didn't they?" Joe said at last, when the cough had worn itself out. "He had to die in Oklahoma."

He wheezed and grunted as Bud hauled him from the brown armchair and put a cane in his hand. They disappeared down the hall. Linda straightened an antimacassar and dumped an ashtray.

"He's been funny today," she told her husband when they were alone. "Walking around with no canes, waving shotguns at people. And then when we were playing cribbage he talked about giving up."

"Giving up what?"

She dodged the truth. "Oh, I don't know. Ranching, maybe."

"Him? Quit ranching? Nah."

Bud sat on the bed and dragged his boots off. Linda pulled a comb through her hair. Glancing in the mirror she thought, "How old I look!"

Out loud she said, "Mardelle Sperry told me they had an offer on their ranch. Six hundred thousand dollars."

Bud tossed one boot into the corner; Linda winced. "We couldn't get that much," he said. He threw the other boot. "And even if we did, after taxes and paying off the mortgages, what'd we have left? No job and no place to live."

Linda pictured a house on a street in town, or even a nice mobile home, with a rosebush, and a pile of paperback books by an easy chair. Whole afternoons of reading—love's tender flame, dangerous delights, happy endings. Grandchildren, perhaps. But somehow she could only see herself alone in this picture, and she hastily pushed the idea away. It was like looking over a cliff.

"If Gordon would come back we could make this place go," said Bud almost harshly.

"Oh, not that again," Linda prayed silently. "Not tonight."

Bud pulled the sheet over himself. "McPhersons have ranched this canyon for over a hundred years. No, Dad doesn't want to leave. Seems full of beans to me."

Lying in the dark, Linda couldn't help retorting: "But there's nothing for Gordon here. Ranching was different when you went to work for your father."

"That's true," said Bud. His voice was full of weariness.

"Joanne likes the ranch," Linda said, her thoughts turning from her son to her daughter.

"It's no job for a girl," scoffed Bud.

Linda kept her disagreement to herself this time. She recalled Joanne's picking herself up out of the dust and manure each time the Appaloosa colt threw her. "She's one of *them*," Linda thought: her alien, unafraid daughter. Beside Linda, Bud lay as familiar as the bed, giving off his masculine scent. She puzzled briefly. Was it shaving cream, sweat, a touch of whiskey, smoke? Her fingertips were stinging from peeling the green chiles that afternoon; when she raised a hand to her nostrils she still caught a whiff of pepper.

Linda was not sleepy. Were the wetbacks hiding under a tree, or hiking north by moonlight? Or fleeing south again?

"Don't worry," her husband murmured. "Nothing's going to happen. Nothing did happen, did it?"

"But it did," Linda thought. "Yes it did!"

"There are no murderers in this canyon," said Bud.

Linda lay for some time watching the silver rectangles in the window frame. At last, knowing that Bud was asleep, she whispered: "Yes there is. Your father!"

That night Joe went riding his horse Champion up into the mountains toward the Pictures. Along the crest of a rock ridge there were several large holes drilled by the wind through the vertical stone, large enough for a horse and rider: if the horse could fly. It was at the base of the Pictures that Joe had shot the lion in the living room. He guided Champion in a switchback pattern up the mountainside, although Champion was such an excellent horse—a good hard animal—that he barely needed the rider's touch. The rocks were loose and jagged underfoot. Remembering the lion hunt, Joe took his time and let the horse calculate his own moves. If the going got too rough Joe must lead on foot, or push from behind. The old man looked high up and saw blue sky burning through the Pictures; he thought of his childhood by the river and how the brown water reflected the color of the clear sky. He remembered gathering wild orchids from the marshes with his cousin, who died young; he thought of Enrique Macías; six wetbacks washed in a bloody pool; Champion stumbled; and they all came rolling down.

Joe gave up, fumbling on the bedside table for his painkiller. Out on the porch the windbells suddenly chattered and battered at one another. Lightning! The old man lay back, bitter medicine in his mouth, and waited for the rain.

# Wild Pigs

## 1

The June sunrise bleached the sky, then reddened it. Monstrous candelabra shapes stood out in the half light. Next a halo of yellowish thorns appeared around each branch. The first whoops and moans of birds were sounding, and nocturnal animals found crannies to hide them through twelve hours in the desert.

## 2

Mrs. Villa's insomnia won out, and she got up.

Her rubber sandals slapped the cool floor. She passed the faded spot on the wall where her husband's picture used to hang, and she switched off a light. She could see the morning paper lying folded in the gray gravel outside. After unfastening the locks and chains, she swung open the kitchen door.

A phantom from her nightmares bolted toward her.

She screamed. Its bristles had scraped her bare knees. Then she fell back against the wall as another beast trampled past. They were snuffling at the kitchen cupboards; she heard their wheezing breath and she smelled a nauseating stench. They must be real.

Mrs. Villa shook off her stupor and groped for the broom.

"Get out!" she shrieked.

## 3

Old Mr. York rose and stood by the window, identifying stars. As usual, his wife slept deeply. A faint Dipper. Polaris. He glimpsed an animal darting through the cactus, but he was too deaf to hear the bird calls. Fifty years ago he had homesteaded this land, half a section of southern Arizona. Down by the river—it flowed in those days—he'd dug a well, built a tiny house, and lived with his wife and child in what was almost a wilderness. Now his property had dwindled to twenty acres.

He turned his eyes to the mountains. Pusch Ridge. Pima Canyon. Castle Rock. In the opposite direction, across the city that still glittered like a bed of electric coals, he could see the long slope of Sentinel Peak and beside it humpbacked Lab Hill, where he had lived as a boy. Soundlessly he finished naming the circle of mountain ranges. Tucson. Santa Rita. Rincon. Catalina. These private incantations never failed to cheer him.

Between parallel lines of clouds the last stars were washing away.

"But of course they're still there," he thought. "We just can't see them."

It was a satisfying idea. Once from the bottom of his well and once again during a total solar eclipse he had witnessed stars in daytime. Sometimes it seemed to Mr. York that everything he knew had changed except for the mountains and the constellations. And with air and light pollution he saw fewer stars even on the darkest nights.

He turned away from the window.

"Wake up, Mother" he said. "Let's take our walk before it gets too hot."

She opened her milky blue eyes and smiled up at him. He had noticed lately that she was sleeping more, and often appeared to answer at random, as though some large internal task preoccupied her.

"How are you?"

"Fine, thank you," she answered dreamily.

They set out after breakfast, the old woman with her coolie hat and walking stick, the old man bareheaded, and the dog. They walked single file along a narrow trail, now sandy, now studded with sharp rocks. Periodically Mrs. York stopped to free her long cotton skirt from the spindly barbed branches of palo verde trees or catclaw bushes. They all stepped automatically around the cactus. The path, followed thousands of times, led first to the mailbox, then down a crumbling bank into a sand wash, and back along the stream bed to their house.

The old man strode ahead, his hands clasped behind his back. The sky had attained a coppery blue and cicadas sent out vibrations from the trees. The Yorks stopped to remove a ball of cactus from the dog, who then applied his nose to the ground and ran ahead of them into the wash.

"Ah, a dry river bed," said Mr. York in a jocular tone, looking down at the creamy breast of sand. "One of Mother Nature's finest feats, a dry river bed."

"Well, she didn't do it by herself, you know," replied his wife.

Fearfully he studied her familiar smiling profile.

They stood at the top of a slope. Most of what had once been their land was sprinkled with houses, irregularly spaced. Between the buildings the wiry trees and bushes remained, and saguaro cacti, all arms and torsos, held up their blackening fruit like burnt-out torches.

The Yorks had sold the land long ago and naively, for little money. In the 1950's they built a second house, and the city grew around them. Traffic drilled along the four-lane road that now formed their eastern property line; the sun set behind the Pizza Inn to the west. From the top of the slope Mr. York tabulated the substances that he could see: rocks, dirt, vegetation, and the perfect curve of the sky. Wood. Brick. Stucco. Tile. Steel. Glass. Plastic. Asphalt.

The original homestead was buried under three-story apartment buildings. Now more apartments were going up, closer.

Mr. York, a civil engineer, had laid out the roads himself, working with transit, rod, and chain fifty years ago. He still took pleasure in their fine straight lines; he liked to see a well-built road with a good surface and freshly painted yellow and white stripes on it.

"The march of civilization," he observed, and he waved his arm toward the town. "Wonderful thing, civilization."

"It's almost over, of course," said Mrs. York.

Suddenly the cry of a siren penetrated even the old man's deafness. Absently probing the path with her stick, Mrs. York seemed to reach a decision, and began to descend into the wash alone. The siren keened in the distance.

"Careful, Mother."

He took one last look at his island of desert and followed her. Halfway down he paused to examine a prickly pear cactus. Between the thorns its dull green skin had apparently been daubed with white paint. Mr. York made a pass at the white material and showed his sticky fingers to his wife. She looked up placidly, having seen this trick before.

He rubbed his thumb and forefinger together. The white pigment was both cottony and granular; the grains were the bodies of insects; they burst and dyed his fingers crimson.

"Cochineal!" he proclaimed.

It was cooler in the wash. They walked beneath palo verde and mesquite trees that sent their tap roots into the invisible stream beneath the sand. Mr. York hoped that he and his wife would die in the same moment, in a bolt of lightning perhaps, before they had to sell their twenty acres. And preferably just before property taxes were due, he reflected. They followed the dog's footprints across the sand, which twinkled darkly with iron magnetite. Then they heard him bark.

The old woman's hand clamped around her husband's bony arm with surprising strength.

"He's got something," she said. "Hurry!"

Hobbling, scrambling, they came around a bend in the stream bed and found the dog. The white fur that caped his neck and shoulders stood on end. He backed slowly toward them, and his barks became growls.

"What is it?" said Mr. York. "A snake?"

"He used to bark like that at the horned owl."

"But it's been gone for years."

"Maybe," Mrs. York whispered, "it's human. Remember—"

Last year they had called the sheriff's department to evict a tramp who was living in the wash.

They strained their eyes in the direction that the dog pointed, but all they saw was a crumbling bank about fifteen feet high. Then, in the shade of some bushes at the bottom, a dim shape moved. The dog let out a howl, and Mrs. York gripped his collar. Another shape appeared.

"Oho," said Mr. York jubilantly. "Javelinas."

The creatures blinked their small eyes and flexed their wet snouts, whirled, and disappeared.

"Well!" Mr. York scanned the bushes for telltale motion, but there was none. He turned to his wife. "I didn't think there were any javelinas left on the homestead."

Now that the crisis was past, he saw that she was drifting away again. She released the dog and looked at the old man with the sweet indifference of a madonna on a monument. Or was her face, he wondered in horror, simply blank?

"Time to go home, Mother," he said, and led the way, identifying rocks.

## 4

The first apartment building had reached the framing stage, while the second was still a jumble of concrete blocks damp with mortar.

The new laborer bent over the Igloo can and filled a paper cup for the fifth time that morning. After drinking noisily, he flipped the cup into the nearest cactus.

"Is it always this hot?" he said.

Sweat varnished his bare back. He pulled a bandanna from his head and wiped himself sketchily, showing no sign of returning to work. Wade, the big carpenter, answered between strokes of his hammer: "No. It'll get hotter."

The new laborer spat a drop of sweat off his upper lip and mumbled something.

"Hey," said Jim, the other carpenter. "Get me a two-by-four."

The new man ambled off toward the lumber pile.

"What's his name again?" asked Jim.

"Mac."

"Over here, Mac. No. Here."

The masons' laborer rattled by with his wheelbarrow, and a quick stare escaped from under his eyelids. The rest of the crew had nicknamed him Sombra because he almost never spoke, although without warning he sometimes whistled a shrill tune unfamiliar to the Anglo workers.

He wheeled his load lightly around a corner and the carpenters continued their work.

"*¡Hijo!*"

"*¡Ay Chihuahua mi tierra caramba!*"

"Spanish," drawled Mac. "How do you like working with these wets?"

"Something's happened," said Wade.

Mac went to look, and when he did not come back, the others followed. Sombra was pointing out into the desert; he chattered, for once.

"*¿Ya ves? Son dos javelinas grandotes.*"

"I don't see nothin'."

"Pigs," said Wade, shading his eyes. "Wild pigs. Under that tree over there."

Their sharp spinal ridges appeared to run from their twisted tails to the moist suction cups of their noses. They were neckless, headless beings, like hairy flounders on edge, with hooves.

"Ugly bastards," said Mac.

"People hunt them," Jim said. "There's a regular season, rifles and pistols. Then musket season—black powder, the whole bit. Then bows and arrows."

One of the masons tossed a stone toward them, and the animals shifted slightly.

"They're almost blind," said Wade.

"I never heard of them before. They don't have 'em in Pennsylvania."

"No." Jim's laugh was like a series of yaps. "Or Michigan."

"There they go," said Wade quietly.

The men started to drift back to their jobs, except for the new laborer, who mopped his neck with his bandanna again, staring out over the olive drab desert.

"Ugliest place I've ever seen," he said. "They ought to blade the whole thing."

## 5

Iris Malone loved ice. She liked the large crystalline cubes that she bought in blue plastic bags, she enjoyed the flatter, whiter ones that her icemaker regularly produced with sepulchral sounds, and she felt a surge of delight every time she pressed a glass against a lever at the front of her new almond-colored refrigerator and watched the glass fill with glittering shards. As a child in Massachusetts she had glutted herself on snow, and she still thought—though perhaps this was simply nostalgia—that a fresh icicle, grasped in a mitten and slowly sucked, had the finest flavor of all.

She held a handful of small cubes over two glasses and let them drop like coins in a wishing well. They tinkled against the slides, splashing as they hit the gin at the bottom. Iris filled her glass with diet tonic water and her husband Bob's with the real thing; she squeezed lime wedges and stirred the drinks with her forefinger. This kind of ice, homemade, was the best to chew. The air bubbles softened it slightly, making it safer for teeth.

She had discovered the sensual joys of grinding ice between her teeth twenty years ago, when the Malones moved to Texas, and later it had helped to ease the burden of many summers and parties lengthened by conversations about computers. California and Colorado weren't as bad as Texas, but Arizona required a lot of ice. And gin.

"Arizona!" she had said when Bob announced the latest move. "It always reminds me of dead jackrabbits."

It was an accurate memory, she found, except that the roadside corpses in Tucson were mainly cottontail rabbits. Of course Texas was littered with mangled armadillos.

"Why is it left to me to notice them?" she wondered, and then answered herself with her usual sedate cynicism: "Because I'm a sport. I'm a sport. I'm a sport."

Iris nudged the patio door open with her knee and carried the drinks outside. Even at six o'clock the heat hit her like a high wind. Executing a turn, Jennifer kicked a shower of water over her parents.

"Watch out, honey," Iris said. She glanced sideways at her husband to see if he were annoyed, but apparently Bob had not noticed the drops that marked his shirt front like tears.

The girl flopped on her back and floated beside them, her blond hair stained dark by the water. Already Jennifer's figure was thickening; she would have to learn to watch her weight, or else she would grow as squat as Bob's mother.

"I was prettier," Iris thought coolly.

"Well!" Bob set his empty glass on the table.

Iris knew that he intended to broach an important topic. Resigned, she looked away and braced herself. An object swirled in the pool near Jennifer's elbow.

"Darling, what's that?"

Jennifer scooped it out, and it lay curled into a C in a puddle at their feet.

"Oh, another drowned lizard," sighed Iris in disgust.

They were not as bad as the sodden kangaroo rats, the hairy, contracted tarantulas, or the scorpions lazily waving their dead tails in the water. Of course, alive they were all immeasurably worse, even the lizards.

"Look, Mom." Jennifer poked curiously at the stiff little body. "Look at his stomach. It's aqua. Like the thinnest leather. And his chin is peach."

"Lovely," said Iris, drinking.

"We have to decide," Bob announced, "what we're going to do next."

And Iris understood that his career with the great electronics corporation had finally leveled off; he would not be promoted again. A bat skimmed across the pool. Iris noticed that at last she felt cooler. Now it was her turn to say, "Well!" If he quit and cashed in his shares of stock, Bob would receive a considerable sum of money, and they could live where they chose.

"I don't want to move," Jennifer said firmly. "I want to finish high school in one place. I like it here."

Bob smiled. "Me too. I don't miss those East Coast winters one bit."

Iris was remembering the fall colors, the spring flowers, the infinity of greens and grays along Cape Cod.

"Well, there's plenty of time to make up our minds," said her husband, disingenuously, she felt.

In the silence they heard a door slam across the road.

"Oh, Mom, I forgot to tell you. Mrs. Villa called this morning, ranting and raving."

"What about?" Iris asked wearily.

Jennifer giggled. "Monsters. Monsters in her kitchen."

Sunset colors, of a vividness that always struck Iris as false, streaked the western sky. Jennifer danced around the pool to get dry. Iris sorted through the ice in her glass and selected a cube. She bit down hard. Then she said through the fragments: "That woman hasn't been all there since he left."

"What?" said Bob. "Your mouth is full." He looked at her hard. "You aren't even aware that you do it, are you?"

Iris ignored him.

"Put some water on the garden, will you, honey?" she called.

At the far end of the pool she had brought in rich soil and planted roses and vegetables—peas, beans, tomatoes, and, for the first time this year, sweet corn, which was impossible to buy in the West. Only that morning Iris had counted the raspy, swelling ears.

"We're supposed to conserve water," Jennifer called back naughtily.

"Jennifer Malone," said Iris, "turn on the hose."

Jennifer's voice rose raggedly from the dusk.

"Mommy, the garden's *gone*!"

The three of them stood together before a small scene of devastation. Of the vegetables, only tumbled cornstalks and a few shredded leaves remained.

"An animal," suggested Bob. "Look, it knocked down the fence." He searched the trampled soil for footprints, and then restated the obvious: "Some large animal."

Jennifer was watching her mother apprehensively. But Iris managed to achieve silence, her glass still clutched in her hand, as alternate waves of heat and cold lapped at the back of her neck. She wondered just how much her share of the Malones' assets would be worth.

## 6

There was a failed storm in the vicinity. By sunset the thick clouds had lifted and coalesced into hemispheres, floating wigs, cauliflowers, sea turtles, and—as they blew over the rim of the planet and headed for California—smoldering galleons sinking into the dark. "Pizza Inn, Pizza Inn," cried the red neon sign from the street below them.

Kay Fielder was sweeping dust into a pile. She was dimly aware of the voices of her husband and children at play in the distance, a summer evening sound, silvery and sad. She swung the broom hard and beat the dust off the brick terrace and onto the ground.

"It's their one good moment," said Charlie, suddenly behind her.

"What?"

He put his arm around her. "Don't be so nervous. The mountains, I mean. Look at the light."

"They have lots of good moments," said Kay.

"Sure, but this is the dramatic one."

Blue shadows hung from the rock faces. Staring upward Kay suffered a flash of the feeling that she privately called "the Helicopter," but this dissipated almost at once.

A high, uncalculated wail rang out. Kay and Charlie found their son and daughter huddled together at the edge of the desert, their eyes fixed on a large greasewood bush. Kay lifted the screaming toddler.

"What is it, Ben?" said Charlie.

"A . . . wolf!" breathed the older child.

"A coyote?" Kay thought of the spring evening when they had witnessed a pack of coyotes at play. They seemed as tall as deer but lighter, and tinged with pink.

"No. Look."

The pair of javelinas poked out their snouts and contemplated the people. Small cleft feet twinkled as they hurried by.

"They're only ten feet away," whispered Charlie.

"They don't see very well," Kay whispered back.

Each of them held a child. The little girl, Ashley, had quit crying. Twigs snapped as the animals rooted under a palo verde tree.

"Do you see the wild pigs?" Charlie asked Ben.

"Peccaries, aren't they?" said Kay. "In zoos they name them for movie stars. Gregory Peccary, Cary Grunt, Zsa Zsa LaBoar."

The animals trotted blindly toward the street.

"What stinks?" exclaimed Ben.

"Musk," said Kay.

They heard the squeal of tires, followed by honking.

"Oh, they're in the road," cried Kay.

Several cars had slowed down or stopped; the javelinas galloped clumsily from one side of the pavement to the other, bewildered by horns, catcalls, and loud clapping. One car flashed its headlights in the dusk. Kay bit her lip. It seemed certain that the animals would be killed, but there was nothing she could do. Ashley clung to her neck. At last the javelinas found themselves on the shoulder of the road; they blundered back onto Kay's property, and, for the moment at least, they escaped.

Groans of disappointment came from the street, and Kay turned away.

"That was great, Mommy. Where did they go? Will they come back?"

"I don't know, Ben." Kay was now exhausted. "It's bedtime."

When the children were asleep Kay and Charlie spread a blanket on the terrace and lay watching stars.

"What's the matter?" said Charlie.

"Nothing."

"You're upset about those damn pigs."

"Peccaries."

"But nobody hit them, did they? They're safe in the desert."

"For how long?" Kay asked bitterly. "Construction is destroying their habitat on all sides. It's just as bad as California."

"You can't afford to take it so hard. It's too big—beyond your control. You'll go crazy that way."

Kay shrank over to her side of the blanket.

You'll go crazy that way.

On the pale green wall, the psychiatrist had hung a large geological map representing a locality unfamiliar to Kay. The only other decorations, besides a potted plant, were a collection of objects arranged on the tabletops and windowsills. They were toys, really—a tiny rocking horse, a clown straddling a ball, a game of steel weights and pendulums, and a set of magnets from which small towers or figures could be built. Kay had made several visits to the office before she decided that the unifying principle here was balance.

Charlie drove her to the doctor and waited outside; he couldn't stand any more tears, he said. She, knowing that each bout brought a period of relief, had resisted treatment. But there she was, telling the doctor about the Helicopter.

She rose alone above the room with the squalling baby in it, above the cracking roof, the skinny trees, the patchy lawns, into the sublimated filth of the smog. She flew higher. She saw swimming pools like fake turquoises, tin beads of traffic shoving one another along the Bloody Bayshore, and, from Foster City all the way down to San Jose, a crust, a vast reef of ticky-tacky houses. And underneath each roof she could see the inhabitants: busy hideous insects, tight with poison juice. The only thing she liked about northern California was the moment when the white fog flooded in slow motion over the hills behind San Francisco.

She sat back, appalled. She sounded crazy to herself. But the doctor glossed over the Helicopter and in practiced phrases he assured her that it was natural to grieve for the way of life she'd lost when she quit her job, married Charlie, moved, and had a baby.

"To oversimplify a bit," he said at last, "you're homesick. Let's see what this medication does for you."

The Helicopter did not disappear, but it changed. She was no longer the pilot but a passenger; she was an accident victim strapped, with her stretcher, onto a pontoon below.

"Feeling better?" asked the doctor.

Kay nodded—hadn't her tears dried up?—and he seemed pleased.

Kay reached out and set one of the pendulums swinging. The toys served another purpose, she realized, in giving uneasy people something to do with their hands. Before this man she felt more naked than she had upon the obstetrician's table. It was during her last visit that the psychiatrist suggested, "Perhaps someday you could move back to Arizona. What's your husband's profession?"

"He's an architect."

"Isn't there lots of growth in Arizona? Jobs for architects?" He smiled across the desk, and Kay hastily dropped her eyes. "Just don't expect perfection if you go home again," he warned in his velvet-padded professional tone.

Charlie settled for a poorer job in Tucson, designing chiropractors' offices and hamburger stands instead of hotels and university buildings. However, he had also designed their new house. His hand groped across the blanket and dragged Kay, protesting, back to his side.

"Be fair," he said. "If this land were never disturbed, the Indians would still be here eating cactus fruit. Your grandfather would never have homesteaded it. You profit from growth and development as much as anybody. For God's sake, what do you think I do all day?"

There was another sensation, which she had never revealed to the psychiatrist; Kay called it the Oppressor. A concrete weight descended upon her chest, squeezing off air, light, sound, movement, and finally feeling. The Helicopter might be endured, even oddly enjoyed, but the Oppressor must be fought.

Charlie sighed. "Change is inevitable. There are limits everywhere. You might as well accept them."

The Oppressor. She forced her lips to move: "Or do something about it."

The Oppressor retreated, and a cube of determination hardened inside her as she waited for sleep. She would do something. But what?

Much later, the scream woke them all. Ashley stood gripping the bars of her crib and sobbing, in the shocking light: "Wolves! Wolves!"

Kay sat for half an hour with the little girl's rigid body on her lap. Finally she turned out the lamp and continued to rock and croon in the dark, as Ashley's arms and legs softened and her joints grew loose. Kay thought of the Helicopter and the Oppressor, and of her grandmother's increasingly bizarre behavior. Chromosomes fumbled toward one another, crossed, and drifted apart on a watery screen in her memory. "What have I given you?" she whispered. She noticed that Ashley was asleep.

Kay walked silently through her house. It was, she admitted, a daring design, perhaps beautiful. She looked out over the desert. In the starlight it appeared dead: sand and driftwood, the end of the world. The Helicopter and the Oppressor seemed far away, but not so far as the psychiatrist.

Kay clenched her fist against the cold window. "Well, I won't be buried alive," she said. "What shall I do?"

She stood there thinking of politics, money, and power — strong and gamy meats that never had tempted her appetite before.

Across the tangled trees and stoic saguaro figures, one yellow pinpoint of light gleamed back at her. Mrs. Villa was still awake, or else she slept with her lights burning. Fatigue seeped along Kay's limbs and into her skull like a drug, driving her to find relief in bed.

## 7

The javelinas slipped through the underbrush. Already gorged on vegetables, they had merely grazed in Kay's garbage can, and now the sand wash drew them back. Several days ago they'd followed the stream bed down from the mountains. The rains were late this year; the city smelled of smoke and water. The javelinas flattened themselves beneath a cactus. Mingled with bird calls at dawn, a bulldozer's backup whistle hooted from the construction site down the hill.

# *Ganado Red*
# *A Novella*

I

# *La Tejedora*

1920

Adjiba Yazzie, also known as La Tejedora, was setting up her loom. Crooning as though to a cradleboard child, she adjusted the vertical warp strings and arranged her balls of yarn upon the ground around her, gray, black, white, and red. She had prepared the raw wool, shorn from the family flock three Mays ago; then she had spun it through the winter nights and dyed the red and black yarn over a fire in front of the hogan the following spring. But the rug had taken a long time to weave.

Adjiba's design was intricate and quite large—six by nine feet. However, the delay had been caused mainly by the epidemic that swept the Navajo reservation in 1918. This disease was far beyond the power of shamans to cure with sings and sand paintings; white people were dying as fast as Indians. Even in their remote settlement the Yazzies had caught it. Adjiba herself lay sick for six days, and her husband Hostin did not leave the hogan for nearly a month. Their daughter Nonobah, who had recently given birth to a baby, died.

Adjiba's fingers flickered automatically through the rough strings of the warp, threading a strand of scarlet yarn over and under, over and under until she reached the end of a red block in her pattern. Then she took up the black. When the row was finished, she beat the new weft threads down hard with a wooden weaver's comb, carved forty years ago by her brother and polished by long use. Her only other tool was a batten, like a wooden knife blade, for manipulating the strings.

Weaving reminded her of Nonobah, whom she had taught. She reached for the gray wool. Horrible spirits hovered around the dead, and it was dangerous to remember them too much, but weaving gave a woman time to think. Again she had a vision of darting flames and rhythmic surges of smoke: they were burning Nonobah's hogan. Well, that was the proper thing to do, a purification. She stopped to count the threads, keeping her pattern exact, and forgot for a moment to grieve.

She could not blame Nonobah's husband for leaving; he was still young, and the Yazzies were not his clan. It was right for her to raise Nonobah's children. Luckily, Adjiba thought, the baby had died too. She beat down the threads with the long-handled comb and started over. The children were becoming useful. They could both herd sheep, and at five Desbah was learning to weave. Adjiba lifted her voice.

"Desbah. Bring me another ball of the red yarn."

The child darted up promptly with the wool, then dropped cross-legged on the sheepskin beside her grandmother.

"Watch how I do it."

Adjiba knotted the new strand to the old, conscious of the young body glowing beside her. Ah, well, I'm not so ancient yet, she said to herself. Desbah and Tsoni could almost have been her own. She thought of her white-haired mother, whose body was as gnarled as a juniper tree. She had lived through the bad times when Kit Carson had scorched the earth and driven half the tribe like sheep on the Long Walk to Bosque Redondo in New Mexico. To Adjiba, who was born after the surviving Navajos were allowed to come home, her mother had spoken little of the ordeal. Once she had said that the Diné, the Navajo people, could not farm in that country: "We were always hungry."

During the epidemic the Yazzies' livestock ran wild and their crops were neglected. The following year their stomachs were often empty, too. But now the sheep looked better, the wool was sold to the trader, and the corn was safely in the ground. If the rains came, and if she got a good price for this blanket, they would be secure until the time to sell sheep in November.

Sitting at the loom, around the cooking fire, or watching the flock, Adjiba's mother had told many other stories: legend and history, both comical and sad. There were accounts of Spider Woman, who, it was said, first showed the Diné how to weave. And once she had recalled a time before the Long Walk, when the Mexicans were in power and used to steal Navajo women and hold them captive to weave. "Slave blankets," the old woman had said with a sour laugh.

"Would you like to try?" Adjiba asked Desbah.

Slowly the little girl poked the yarn along the row. Adjiba tweaked it and gave a nod of approval. They were all good weavers in her family, she told her granddaughter, beating the threads down. When the work was done the colored weft threads would conceal the warp entirely.

"Watch me now," she said.

They sat there without speaking while Adjiba wove a stripe as wide as her thumb. She was happy when spring came and she could work outdoors under the broad blue sky, with a prospect of cottonwood trees startling the eye: fresh light green against the cinnamon sand. When the woman stopped to count threads the child asked, "How can you remember it all?"

Adjiba laughed. She saw the design in her head first, while she was preparing the wool, she answered.

"You will start with simple forms," she said. "First maybe a striped saddle blanket. As you grow older, the harder ones will come."

Oh, it was wrong, she thought, when the young were taken before the old, leaving patterns incomplete. But in a way time brought harmony again. She took up her wool and filled in a small white triangle. The light was growing weaker, she noticed, and she began to hear the sounds of the flock coming home for the night. Bells clanked, and the goats, newborn lambs, and old rams protested high and low in their wordless voices.

Tsoni pounded up behind them on a thin spotted horse with bulging eyes and stopped in a shower of sand.

"Don't ride like that," his grandmother scolded.

He slid to the ground.

"Women own sheep but men own horses," he said importantly.

"Men?" jeered Desbah.

Adjiba saw with satisfaction that his arm and leg bones were stretching out, apparently leaving his childish body behind. She had observed that during bad times the children failed to grow. With calculated flattery, Tsoni admired the rug on the loom.

"When it's finished, can I go with you to Hubbell's to sell it?"

"Who'll watch the sheep?" she asked.

"My uncle. It's only four days."

"Maybe longer."

"Can I?"

"Perhaps. And maybe Desbah, too. She's helped me with the weaving."

Tsoni let out a whoop and hurled himself upon the nervous horse. The grandmother sighed. She had several more months of work, she estimated, if all went well. She laid the comb and batten side by side and gathered herself up from the ground.

Late in August, Juan Lorenzo Hubbell was sitting under a cottonwood tree by the riverside, watching a small cloud slip across the sky. Seated in rocking chairs, both he and his oldest son, Lorenzo, were drinking strawberry soda pop. The Pueblo Colorado Wash had run recently but was now dry, revealing a bed of pink sand eroded into a miniature version of the Four Corners landscape—buttes, mesas, canyons, and braiding streams.

With a characteristic gesture the old man smoothed his white mustache, which was already as straight as a coarse clean paintbrush. Before him lay a long sandstone fortress of a building, part warehouse and part hacienda. It was the Hubbell Trading Post, the capital of his empire.

"Did you go to the Snake Dance this summer?" Hubbell asked suddenly.

"No," said Lorenzo, draining his bottle. "I didn't make it."

They watched the clouds thicken over the cornfield. Twenty years earlier Hubbell had settled here and named the straggling village Ganado, Arizona after a Navajo friend of his, the chief Tiene Mucho Ganado. Now there were fourteen Hubbell trading posts, including the one that Lorenzo managed at Oraibi on the nearby Hopi reservation.

Gradually the two men became aware of a distant noise.

"Indians," said Hubbell.

They could see the open wagon bouncing slowly across the wooden bridge. A pair of bony spotted horses dragged their load up to the trading post, and the Navajo passengers climbed down and beat the dust from their clothes.

Hubbell squinted through his small steel-rimmed spectacles.

"Why, it's La Tejedora," he said. "I haven't seen her for years."

"Maybe she's brought in a blanket," said Lorenzo, helping his father to rise. Once up, the old man shook off Lorenzo's hand and started up the hill to the post.

"*Ya-at-eeh*, Tejedora," he called.

She turned, and they saw beneath the pale powdering of dust a square, vigorous woman with almost Japanese features. Doubled and redoubled, then bound with red yarn at the back of her neck, her black hair still made a thick bundle. She thumped herself on the chest, smiling; her silver necklace danced, and a cloud of dust rose from her purple velvet blouse. In spite of the warm weather she was wrapped in a bright Pendleton blanket. A little girl, also wearing the traditional velvet blouse and crinkled skirt to the ankles, thrust herself behind the woman as the Hubbells came near.

"*Ya-at-eeh*, Hostin," said Lorenzo to the driver of the wagon, who was hitching the horses to a rail beside the low front door. "Have you come far today?"

Adjiba Yazzie's husband ducked his head affirmatively. It was his habit to agree with whatever a white man said, even the familiar Hubbells who spoke Navajo. It saved trouble, Hostin thought; Adjiba sometimes had her doubts. But she, too, allowed the Hubbells to call her "Tejedora"—"Weaver" in Spanish—instead of using her Navajo name.

"Take the team around to the stable," Hubbell said.

Tsoni, suddenly subdued, followed his grandfather. Adjiba placed a hand on Desbah's back and propelled her gently through the doorway after the Hubbells. The narrow door squeaked shut, cutting off the powerful sunlight. They stood in the "Bull Pen," a long room with an uneven wooden floor, encircled on three sides by counters higher than Desbah's head. Every crevice was stuffed with merchandise. The little girl froze, except for her dark eyes, which rolled from the candy jar to the piñon pine beams overhead, hung with horse collars.

"Come in, come in," cried Lorenzo casually. "Want a bottle of pop?"

Desbah was too shy to take it from him, so Adjiba put it into her hand. Lorenzo watched the child's expression as she tasted the garish pink liquid and sneezed.

"First time?" he laughed.

He was the fattest man Adjiba had ever seen, with a thick neck and a forty-eight inch waist. She studied him frankly. During the hard times he seemed to have gained weight. But of course he was always surrounded by food.

A pyramid of canned peaches rose behind his head. On the shelves beyond the counter she glimpsed other cans: tomatoes, corned beef, pears, and condensed milk. She could tell what they were by the pictures on the labels, though the cow on the milk can had once seemed confusing. Back in the corners gleamed new tin washtubs and pails and glass chimneys for kerosene lamps. Spurs, bits, bridles, and other tack were displayed directly in front of Adjiba, but she moved toward the counter that she liked best and stood there soaking in the colors. Skeins of commercial yarn sprawled from a basket; spools of thread were arranged by tone. Bolts of calico leaned against the wall, and lengths of velvet were specially hung to avoid crushing the nap.

"It's been a long time, Tejedora," said Hubbell. "Are these Nonobah's kids? Where's Nonobah?"

Adjiba stretched out her hand and the old man grasped it for a moment. Then she turned back to the yarn, tears in her eyes, and he sank onto a small bench beside the woodstove that occupied the center of the room.

"I've been sick too, Tejedora," he said. "I'm sorry."

Hostin and Tsoni entered the store, carrying a bundle wrapped in a flour sack. The boy stared accusingly at his sister, and Adjiba murmured, "Give him one, too."

No one spoke for several minutes. Hostin set the bundle down and examined some ax handles. The children cautiously drank their strawberry soda pop, stingingly sweet.

Finally Lorenzo said, "Are you going to bring us some sheep in November?"

"Yes," said Hostin.

"These new sheep," continued Lorenzo chattily, "have more meat but the wool's not so good."

Hostin agreed.

Hubbell said, "Is that a blanket, Tejedora?"

She nodded.

"Good! There's been practically a famine of blankets for the past two years," he told her. "You're lucky that Lorenzo's here. He's handling all that side of the business now, at Oraibi."

She nodded again, looking from one man to the other. The Hubbells, being half Mexican, were not as strangely colored as a trader she remembered from Keam's Canyon, who had red, speckled skin, blue eyes, and orange hair that curled like a sheep's.

"But maybe you heard that already," said Hubbell. He heaved himself to his feet. "Bring it on into the rug room."

Adjiba followed him down one step into a cluttered office and then through another door into a small room lined with bookcases, which were nearly concealed by stacks of Navajo rugs. She unfolded hers on the floor at Hubbell's feet.

"Ay, Tejedora," said Lorenzo from the doorway, "so this is what you did with all that red dye I sold you!"

She smiled a little nervously. Hubbell rubbed a corner of the rug between his fingers. "Very nice," he said. "You're a good weaver, *Tejedora*."

She was embarrassed and looked away. Above the bookcases Hubbell had hung a number of small paintings of old rugs with designs that he liked, as models for the weavers. The women rarely copied a picture exactly but drew on them for ideas.

"It's a big one," observed Lorenzo. "Good pattern. Good straight edges, nice and tight. But so very red."

"Well, I like red," said his father calmly. "It's traditional."

In the old days, before American traders came with their dyes and their readymade yarn, the Navajo weavers used to obtain red wool by ravelling a coarse English cloth called baize, or *bayeta* in Spanish.

Lorenzo switched to a mixture of English and Spanish. "That man at Fred Harvey's is always asking for gray blankets with a little red, not red ones with a little gray."

"It's a good piece of weaving. Just give her less money for it."

Lorenzo hesitated, glancing at the silent woman kneeling beside the red rug. Adjiba sensed that the Hubbells were discussing some flaw in the work that affected the price; she folded her hands with resignation and stared at the three lumps of turquoise in her bracelet. Hubbell suppressed his impatience with his son, whose heart had an unpredictable way of going soft. Now that Lorenzo was in charge, was he keeping his accounts straight? The old man smoothed his mustache and spoke: "You decide."

"One hundred dollars, Tejedora," Lorenzo said in Navajo.

A broad smile escaped before she could cover her mouth with her hand. One hundred! It was the most she'd ever received.

"Prices are up," explained Lorenzo, more to his father than to her.

"Very well," said Hubbell. "Now come with me, Tejedora. I want to show you some rugs in my house."

Adjiba had never entered the rooms at the back of the trading post where the Hubbells lived. The first thing she noticed was the fine rug beneath her feet. Then she raised her eyes and was shocked by the amount of space. How lonely these people must feel, she thought, in such a long empty place. She felt very far from the comfortable shadows of her hogan. Under the dome of logs and mud there was room for a family to sleep around the fire and to keep a few possessions—a pot, a quilt, a bunch of dried herbs, an enameled dishpan. She could set up a small loom. With the light that fell through the smoke hole, they had no need of windows.

"Come along, come along, Tejedora." Hubbell stumped ahead.

This central hall and living room was actually full of antique furniture, mounted animal heads, pictures in gold frames, and Indian artifacts. The rugs, however, were the most striking feature. Both huge and small, patterned in red, gray, black, brown, blue, and white, they covered the floor. Adjiba gaped; she would never spread one upon the dirt floor of her hogan. Here, rugs were also draped over furniture and made into cushions. So this was what white people did with them. She wondered briefly where her red rug would go.

"Look," said Hubbell. He pulled a long thin runner from the top of an upright piano and showed her a design of interlocking combs. Then he ran his hand over the piano keys and smiled at her amazement. Last he led her into another room, where an intricate brass bed was covered with a silky twill blanket, golden brown.

"This," he told her, "is where President Teddy Roosevelt slept when he visited me."

Adjiba nodded. The comb design, she thought, was interesting.

She was glad to see Hostin and the children again, back in the Bull Pen. He had already chosen a new coat; she still preferred to wear a blanket, though not one of her own making. With a few exceptions she wove only for sale. Commercial cloth was so much softer. . . . She touched a fold of Prussian blue velvet and remembered that it used to be Nonobah's favorite color.

Tsoni and Desbah were eating Cracker Jack.

"How do you want it, Tejedora? Cash or credit?" asked Lorenzo.

"Credit." What use would cash be?

He began to write up her account:

| *La Tejedora.* | *Aug. 28, 1920.* | *Fancy Ganado Red.* | *$100.00.* |
|---|---|---|---|
| 2 Soda Pops | | | .40 |
| 2 Cracker Jack | | | .40 |
| Coat | | | 2.00 |
| Peaches | | | .40 |
| 3 Axe Handels | | | 1.50 |
| 8 # Spuds | | | .40 |
| 1 # Coffee | | | .31 |

She added a pair of sheep shears, a sack of flour, a can of baking powder, and a packet of tobacco.

"Is there anything you want to get out of pawn?" asked the trader.

Adjiba shook her head.

"Tin?"

Hubbell issued his own tin money, redeemable at all his trading posts. But with another negative sign she moved to the dry goods counter and caressed the Prussian blue velvet again. A yard would make a fine new blouse for a little girl, she thought. She also chose a red silk handkerchief for Tsoni, and she stood for some time in silence before the yarns and dyes.

Hostin went outside. Lorenzo dropped penny candy into the children's open hands.

A picture of Adjiba's next rug was growing in her mind, with a pinkish sandstone brown as the main color. She remembered her mother's recipe for that—mountain mahogany root, boiled with juniper or spruce branches and rock salt. But black for the border and details was the hardest shade to make at home.

"Three packages," she said, pointing at the black dye.

For contrast she could see natural white wool. She would work out the full design tomorrow. As the wagon wheels turned and turned, through the sage, past cliffs, across dry river beds, she would be imagining her pattern. Then she would hold the picture inside her head, both in general composition and row by row, until she loosened the tension rope and cut the finished work from the loom.

Smiling, Adjiba gathered up her purchases.

And somewhere, she thought, there must be a touch of green.

II

# *The Collection*

1924

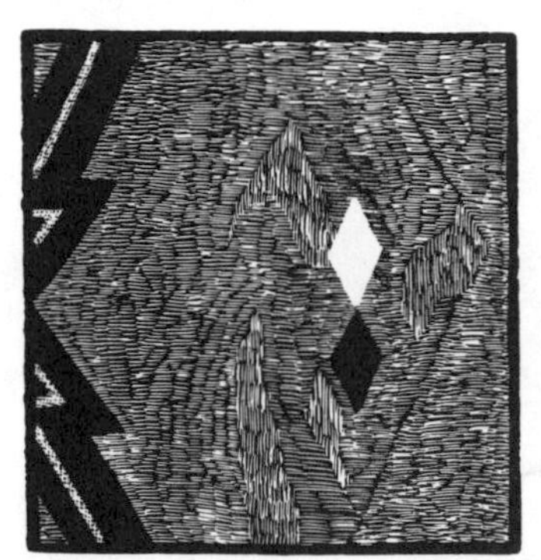

Hazel McFarland steered the Packard in a wide arc around the cottonwood tree and stopped. From beneath the grape arbor, where she suspected that he had been dozing, appeared rumpled Don Cuco, the gardener. She set the handbrake and climbed out. Her older sister Henrietta had never learned to drive, but Hazel rather enjoyed it. She sucked in a breath of tonic Santa Fe air; as usual it was perfumed with piñon pine smoke. The sisters had lived in New Mexico since the end of the Great War, finding much the same glamour here as in Italy, with less expense and trouble.

Don Cuco moved without haste to the great front door and pulled it open for Hazel, sketching a bow. Really, she thought, even he was quite courtly! He stood in the open doorway and stared after her until she said, "*Gracias, Don Cuco,*" twice.

She waited for the slightly fibrous cedar door to close before she unpinned her brown felt hat. It was too much like disrobing in front of him. Etta would probably think so, anyway. Hazel peered at the dim round face in the mirror—with the door shut, the entry was poorly lighted—and gave her hair a few ineffectual pushes. Its heavy coils were starting to slip out of their knot. She sighed.

"Hazel?"

"Yes."

"I'm in the Gallery."

That tortuous silver gilt mirror frame ought to surround the image of a Baroque saint, Hazel thought, not a graying spinster from the Midwest. The sisters' Santa Fe house contained a hodgepodge of treasures, both Southwestern and European. Like many an amateur museum it was imperfectly zoned by subject or period. The silver gilt mirror consorted oddly with a barbaric Spanish trunk, its cowhide peeling like bark from a dead tree; an African mask; a jar of peacock feathers; and a late Victorian portrait in oils of their father, a St. Louis soap millionaire with pince-nez.

Hazel descended a few picturesque but uneven brick steps, passed through an arched opening in the thick adobe wall, and came upon her sister. Western sun streamed through the high windows here, silhouetting the angles of Etta's figure. Apparently struggling with an arrangement of flowers, she cried out in pain or annoyance.

"That man!" she said. "That gardener will not remove the thorns for me."

"Perhaps he doesn't understand," said Hazel.

"Oh, I think he does. What's the word for thorn? *Espina*?"

"Well, it's natural for roses to have thorns," said Hazel vaguely. Etta snorted, gave the flowers one more twitch, and dusted off her hands.

"Did you get the shopping done?" she asked.

"He was out of meat for the day."

Etta flung herself into a low plush armchair. "What a bore. All we have is eggs for supper, and Artemisa is still gone. But then what took you so long?"

Hazel touched one of the rose petals with the tip of her forefinger. Like flocked paper, she thought, only finer, and alive. Or once alive. She bent over the vase and touched the red petals with her lips.

"Hazel?"

"Oh," she said, "I stopped by the Shalako Shop, too."

"Anything interesting?"

"Well," said Hazel, temporizing. "Maybe."

"Were there any Acoma pots? Or new kachina dolls?"

Hazel did not think so. "Harold Granger was there, down from Taos," she said.

"Seedy little fellow," snapped Etta. Then after a moment she prompted; "Well, what sort of monkey tricks are going on in Taos?"

Hazel sat opposite her. "There's been a big party given by Mabel Dodge Sterne, or whatever she calls herself. Harold says she's married that Indian and added the name Luhan now."

"No!"

"Yes, and she invited all the Indians from the pueblo to the party, and everyone danced. Everyone was there, Willa Cather, Mary Austin, Leon Gaspard, Ralph Meyers . . . all drunk."

She let Etta savor the news and then added, "If we were ever invited to one of her parties, would you go?"

"Certainly not," said Etta. "We collect Indian artifacts, but she collects Indians."

Hazel, looking around the Gallery, imagined the glass cases full of lithe brown bodies instead of painted pottery and ceremonial objects. She saw a black-haired man, nearly naked, wearing the Sioux war bonnet hung on the wall. She saw hands beating the furry Apache drums, human forms wrapped in the Navajo rugs, and a baby wailing in the elaborate cradle-board. Then she suppressed a nervous hiccup.

"Speaking of artifacts," she began, "I did see something at the Shalako. In fact I bought it."

As she had expected, her sister was surprised and rather offended. Usually they shopped together and Etta made the final decisions.

"I'm glad you're finally taking an interest in the Collection," Etta said coldly. Her curiosity rose, and she asked, "What is it?"

"A blanket—a rug, really."

"Oh, another rug. Wherever shall we put it?"

"I don't know," said Hazel, feeling her dismay growing. For an instant she wondered if Mr. Furnival at the Shalako Shop would take it back.

"And where is it?"

"I left it in the Packard," said Hazel unhappily. "It's a bit bulky."

"Well, let's have it in, shall we?" Etta leaned out one of the French doors leading from the Gallery to the terraced gardens. "Cuco! Cuco!" she sang out at a pitch far above her speaking voice. It was her imperative calling voice, and it first produced two Irish wolfhounds.

"How are you, my darlings? Darling Cuchulain, swee-test Brian Boru." And then again she shrieked, "Cuco! Cuco!"

Don Cuco parted the leaves of the hedge and gazed up at her.

"Come here, if you please," she called.

He sidestepped through the Haida totem poles and slowly climbed the garden steps to the terrace. Then he removed his battered straw hat and stood before her without blinking. Hazel noticed that the three days' growth of beard on his chin was dashed with silver.

"Cuco, Miss Hazel has left a parcel in the motor. Bring it in, please."

"*Por favor*," mumbled Hazel, trying not to catch his eye. Then, as her sister closed the French door, Hazel had a cheering thought. She had forgotten the best news of all.

"He told me all about the Lawrences, Etta."

She had never quite understood her older sister's fascination with the world of high culture. They lived a conventional life at its fringes, occasionally peeking in like children at a grown-up party. Their father had brought many paintings back from his Grand Tour, so Etta's mania for collecting could be considered as legitimate an inheritance as her fortune. But he had had a taste for Dutch still lifes and landscapes; she ranged wider. And Hazel trailed behind.

Their mother's family had intellectual connections in New England, and she had been clever and restless. Etta was said to take after her; no one ever expected brilliance from Hazel, the baby of the family, and she never exhibited it. Of course girls need not go to college at the turn of the century. There was also a brother, who was sent to Harvard and made a mess of it and everything else he attempted. Now Eliot's money was fully separated from his sisters': Etta had seen to that; she had financial aptitude. But, perhaps unfortunately, she showed no interest in the business of soap.

"So Lawrence *is* back," Etta breathed.

"I wonder if we'll catch a glimpse of him this summer," said Hazel, watching Etta's expression. Her thin, dry skin was stretched tightly in anticipation across her cheekbones, making her look almost girlish. If she were cut, Hazel wondered inadvertently, would she bleed? Or would it be like slashing a withered piece of fruit—mere stickiness?

Etta would have nothing to do with Eliot now. He was depraved, diseased, she said. When Hazel mentioned the names of Byron and Baudelaire, Etta only said, "Our brother is no poet." Privately Hazel felt that Eliot was far from crazy. They had each been supplied equally. Eliot's spectacular bonfire was now dying, while the sisters only threw on a log at a time. And pooled, their funds would last even longer. Hazel slipped off to visit him sometimes in New York.

"The Lawrences," she said, "are living up at the Del Monte Ranch. Mrs. Sterne—Luhan—gave it to him in exchange for a manuscript. And another woman lives there too, an English noblewoman, in a *ménage à trois*. But Mrs. Lawrence makes her sleep in the outhouse, which *he* has painted with a great coiled snake. They're painting everything. Obscene pictures."

"Of what?" asked Etta, her eyes bright.

"Harold didn't say. And the English lady wears a sombrero, leather trousers, and a dagger in her boot."

"Good heavens!"

"Mrs. Lawrence dresses like a German peasant. And *he* does the housework, bakes bread, scrubs floors, milks the cow. Did I tell you that the Englishwoman is deaf? She carries a brass ear trumpet everywhere, holding it under people's noses."

"What she must hear!"

"Yes, the Lawrences fight like the Kilkenny cats, he said. Everyone is jealous of everyone else. Once Lady What's-her-name cut off Mabel Dodge's ear."

"How on earth?"

"They were bobbing one another's hair."

"The cut direct!" laughed Etta. She was in a thoroughly good mood again, Hazel saw.

"I wonder what he's writing on top of the mountain. I like his books so much better than Mr. Joyce's," she ventured.

During the previous winter, not without some feelings of naughtiness, the sisters had obtained *Ulysses* and each had attempted to read it.

"That's just because you don't understand Joyce," said Etta.

"Is it?"

"I find Lawrence's meaning only too clear."

"Do you?" retorted Hazel. An old indignation sprang up inside her, and her sister, agitated, turned away. As though a dye were soaking through parchment, a slow flush stained Etta's cheeks and throat. So she could bleed after all, Hazel thought.

In Florence, just before the war, Hazel was married for a week. The man was Italian: Riccardo Vivarini. Hazel used to sit alone in her room and practice the rich syllables. She would also whisper to herself, "La baronessa Vivarini, la baronessa Vivarini."

They had taken a villa for the season, Hazel and Etta and Papa. Not the choicest of villas, it lacked any particular view, either of the Fiesolan hills or Brunelleschi's dome, and the marble floors were dank in February. Mamma had loved Florence and wouldn't have tolerated the Villa Cenerentola for a moment. Would she have accepted Riccardo as a son-in-law? Alone in her room afterward, Hazel sometimes wondered. But when it happened, Etta and Papa were in charge, and Papa was ill; the glossy, black, hard-paunched form in his portrait was gradually deflating.

"Where can that man have got to?" Etta exclaimed.

Hazel listened to the clack of her sister's wooden heels striking the tiled floor. Oh, Riccardo, she thought, painfully aware of her own foolishness. She recalled the words that he had whispered in her ear as they strolled among Michelangelo's Schiavi, those human blocks of stone. She kept trying to avert her eyes from the white male figure of David, which stood above and beyond them in a small apse. At thirty, tongue-tied, never pretty, she believed it was her only chance. And then: the elopement, that dusty week in the Tuscan countryside until her money ran out, seven days, six nights. Once they had dined upon sausages in the farmhouse where Machiavelli spent his exile, within sight of the thrusting orange cathedral dome—"*la Hupola*," Riccardo called it, in his Florentine accent.

Soon afterward came her family's accusations, Riccardo's disappearance, and, eventually, the annulment. Presenting the various pieces of evidence, Etta told her, "I'm only doing this because I love you."

"Me or my money?" The words flashed through Hazel's head, but she was too oppressed to utter them. It was the only time she had ever known Etta to use that potent phrase.

*Let me count the ways.* Riccardo had found many in Italian, Hazel remembered. (Etta had no ear for languages.) But Elizabeth Barrett Browning had eloped to Florence, not out of it, and had a baby too, she thought confusedly.

"A libertine. An adventurer. In fact, an abductor."

It was curious, given the way that Etta's mind worked, that she could find delight in a fake Botticelli panel of Cupid and Psyche, or even in a pre-Columbian fertility goddess. Actually the primitive seemed to satisfy her most. She had very little taste for modern art. In Italy she had collected mostly examples of the pre-Renaissance, including some dubious and graceless works "of the school of Cimabue."

After Riccardo was vanquished they returned to St. Louis; war broke out in Europe; Papa died in 1916. Etta had already begun to order Indian handicrafts from catalogues, and by the time they took their first trip to New Mexico Hazel guessed that they would never go back to Italy.

"Ah," cried Etta in relief, "here he comes."

Don Cuco deposited a thick red, white, gray, and black cylinder at Hazel's feet, which retracted from it.

"*Gracias, Don Cuco,*" she said, and he left without a second hint.

"Why do you call him 'Don?' " asked Etta a trifle too loudly. "Is he Don Juan? Don Quixote?"

"The maids do," Hazel said meekly. "I think it's out of respect for his age."

"But you need not respect him—or his age either."

"No, I suppose not," said Hazel, starting to unroll the rug. When the full fifty-four square feet were spread out, she looked up at her sister for comment.

"Good heavens! It's red!"

"Ganado red," said Hazel.

"Terribly red."

"According to Mr. Furnival at the shop, it's by one of the best weavers at the Hubbell Trading Post in Ganado."

Etta bent over and tugged at the edge. Then she examined the tightness of the weave and matched the corners to see if the rug were symmetrical.

"It is good work," she conceded. "But the color!"

"Look at the design," urged Hazel.

Within a solid black border, its basic unit was a small triangle. From thousands of triangles the weaver had constructed a graduated pattern that reached its climax in the center of the rug, where a field of deep scarlet surrounded a black and a white triangle, tip to tip.

"There," said Etta shrewdly, "she tells us what she's doing."

After this moment of simplicity, or mischief perhaps, the design resumed its intricacies. As a composition it was both bold and labyrinthine.

"Turkish carpets are red," suggested Hazel.

"Yes. But where could we put it? It would clash with what we've got. And how much did you pay for it?

"Three hundred dollars," Hazel confessed.

"Why, that's as much as a Persian carpet. Hazel, how could you?" Hazel dropped her eyes to the floor; the rug caught and held them. It was as good as watching a fire. She thought that she would like to lie upon it and soak the color into her bones, as others, more daring, lay in the sun.

"I shall keep it in my room," she said.

"But you already have Mamma's Aubusson."

Hazel stooped and with trembling hands rolled up the rug again.

"I don't care," she said.

"Hazel!"

The rug was not very bulky after all, she found.

"It's just as much my money as yours," Etta cried oddly after her. "I saved it for you, didn't I?"

Saved what, thought Hazel, hurrying through the dark hall. What if she simply drove away? Maybe Lawrence would take her in, too. She stumbled over the Spanish trunk—Etta also had a passion for containers: chests, boxes, baskets, and urns—and stopped to find the light switch. On top of the mountain, she thought, the Lawrences were living with oil lamps. She could imagine the poor Englishwoman seated at the very edge of the circle of light.

There was a noise in the kitchen.

"Artemisa?" called Hazel.

Their cook had been missing since the previous evening. Hazel dropped the rug and went to investigate. The noise came again, but it had nothing to do with the comfortable sounds of cooking. Instead she thought that perhaps one of the dogs was whimpering in the kitchen. She pushed open the door and discovered a pair of embracing figures in the half light.

"Excuse me," she stammered.

They dropped their arms, and she recognized Viola the maid and Artemisa the cook, both weeping. Hazel retreated a step and asked what was the matter. She noticed a flaming weal across Artemisa's normally placid olive features.

"*Su novio*," said Viola reproachfully, though whether of Hazel or the man, Hazel could not tell. She hadn't even known that Artemisa had a sweetheart.

"I'm sorry," she said, embarrassed. "Don't bother about supper, Artemisa, please. We'll just cook some eggs."

"I will do it," said Viola, crossing her hands dramatically on her breast.

"Very well, thank you, Viola."

Hazel had not realized that it was possible for eggs to burn. After a stony meal she escaped to her room. The explanation for Artemisa's absence had not appeased Etta much, and Hazel foresaw more explosions. She closed her bedroom door and leaned against it. The moon was rising across her window like a mother-of-pearl lure at the end of an invisible line.

Hazel unrolled the Navajo rug over the flowery Aubusson carpet. Then she sank down upon it and began to pluck pins from her head. Across the room, in the mirror of the heavy English dressing table, she saw a wild squaw hunched behind her hair.

A sequence of thoughts, cool and clear, came into her mind. Etta would get over it; she always did. As if by telescope Hazel apprehended the pattern of their life together. She closed her eyes. She was three years old, and Etta was pushing her on a swing. Higher and higher she soared, each time into a marvelously fearful place where she could almost let go and fly, but never did. She fell back toward Etta, and Etta pushed her again.

Hazel opened her eyes and let them wander around her room. The closet concealed other rebellions: a lilac satin picture hat, a too-bare bathing costume, an old doll, and rows of elegant, painful shoes.

"If he were honest, he would not disappear," Etta had argued.

Hazel stared at the moon through her long hair. Where was Riccardo now? Etta had liked him, too, at first; Hazel remembered her sister's excited smile when he arrived to escort them through the sights of Florence.

"Maybe not a baron, but more than a guide," Hazel whispered.

Then ten years of opaque resentment parted like a cloud, and a dazzling new thought presented itself. Why, Etta was jealous. Of what? Hazel frowned as she laboriously followed the thought to its end: jealous of them both. Once something joined the Collection, Etta expected it to stay where she had placed it. "No Navajo rugs in the bedrooms," Hazel said to herself. "Or lovers." She began to shiver.

The whitewashed beehive fireplace in the corner lay empty. Hazel moved across the rug and lifted the lid of a Renaissance marriage coffer that Etta had decided she didn't quite like. Almost as long as Hazel was tall, it was painted with swags of fruit and flowers surrounding the figures of Ruth and Naomi, whimsically flanked by cherubs. Hazel fished out a shawl.

When she sat down again, the moment of clarity had passed. Words and pictures flickered through her head in their usual disorder. Artemisa's face. A dog on a lead. She remembered her last night with Riccardo. At dawn she had awakened with a jerk; she was drowning, but there was no water. Then in the weak light squeezing through the shutters she saw that one of his hands, sprouting black hairs, was clasped around her neck.

So Etta was jealous. What difference did that make? Hazel fixed her eyes on the gray, black, and white triangles which danced around her in a pool of blood. And when she looked up, the person in the mirror was not Hazel but D. H. Lawrence, wrapped in a blanket and crowned with feathers.

The moon had set.

I must have slept, Hazel thought dimly. She took a step toward the dressing table, recognizing her own silver-backed comb and brush upon it, and a pair of scissors.

She raised them slowly to eye level and began to cut. She heard a sound like the tearing of silk, and hanks of brown and white hair slipped to the floor.

The woman in the jagged bob put her hands to her cheeks and began to cry.

## III

# *The Castle of the Fairy Queen*

1980

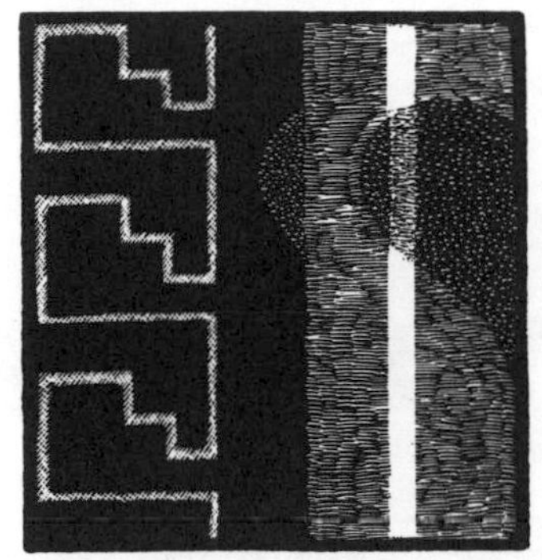

Roger Biscay found the pueblo of San Fulano lying apparently deserted beneath a film of dust. He knew, however, that behind the black windows many eyes were probably watching him. Sunny's directions to the place she called "the Castle" had been accurate so far. As the car rocked slowly through the sandy ruts, one inhabitant of the pueblo lifted itself from the shadows and came toward him, snarling. A yellow dog.

Roger had been here before. Half unwillingly, because at that time they were not fully reconciled, he'd come with his father to a ceremonial dance. These chunky buildings screened a plaza, he remembered. Trembling on the verge of giggles, young girls in fringed white dresses waited to perform. They waved branches of green leaves. An old drummer chanted, ignoring the self-conscious tourists. Under a ramada, pinto beans and *carne seca* simmered, and Roger recalled the odor of frying fat, somewhere between savory and rank. Afterward, the display of pottery had been disappointing.

He stamped on the accelerator and, tasting dust, left the dog behind.

Turn left at the old water tank, Sunny had said on the telephone. Five years evaporated at the sound of her voice, still broken by odd squeaks: "Roger! What are you doing in Santa Fe?"

"A buying trip for the shop," he said. "I've been to an auction."

It was not his first trip to Santa Fe in five years, merely the first time he had called her.

"Far out!" She seemed to fill his ear with laughter, which, considering how they had parted, was intriguing. "You have to come to San Fulano to see me; I haven't got a car. Can you come this afternoon? We're having like a party. But how did you know where I was?"

"I ran into Veronica," Roger said.

"Oh. I haven't seen her in ages. I've been living in the country. It's fantastic."

There was the old water tank, balanced on its rotting legs like the carcass of a spider. "Three miles down the road, across a cattle guard, turn right. One mile to the Castle." He felt as susceptible as ever to the romance of the road.

Just past the water tank the road divided in two. Roger stared. The two forks seemed equally well traveled; there was no sign. He glanced in the rearview mirror, but all he saw was a creamy brown plume of settling dust, his own. Now this was more like Sunny, he said to himself. Clearly the wisest course led down neither fork but home to Tucson, his business, and his wife.

After the auction he had intended to check out of his hotel. Then he'd come upon Veronica, standing outside the French pastry shop in the lobby. She wore a gray business suit and carried a briefcase; her hair, which had hung to her waist in 1975, was now cut short.

The new Veronica, chewing puff paste, still set his teeth on edge. The pottery shop where he had met her and Sunny had long since closed, she said.

"So I went to work for the state of New Mexico. Social services planning. You knew I had a degree in sociology, didn't you? By the way, did you ever get your Ph.D.?"

He pushed away the thought of that abandoned project. "I run the family business now. Indian arts."

"Oh." Veronica licked her fingers and eyed him. "Seen Sunny lately?"

Roger shook his head.

"A lot of water under the bridge," she offered, and he could only agree.

"Well," said Veronica comfortably, "she's left that Indian, of course, and she's living out near San Fulano. She does some kind of craft."

"What Indian?" he said before he could stop himself.

"You didn't know?" Verionica ripped her second croissant in half. Chocolate oozed out. "Well, soon after you left, she ran off to the reservation with this Zuñi. Joe, his name was. Or maybe he was a Laguna. Anyway, Sunny was madly in love, full of Indian lore. Indians were better than Anglos in every way: sex, medicine, morality, religion. You know."

"But it didn't last?"

"Oh, no." She searched her plate for more crumbs. "They didn't have indoor plumbing, and he made her carry water, chop wood, and take care of the animals. And then he beat her. And he told her that she'd never understand Indians. Of course," Veronica added smugly, "she only took one anthropology course, and she never got a degree in anything."

At last Roger detached himself, thinking that the State of New Mexico must be lenient about lunch hours, and she tapped away on her high heels.

The perpetual sidekick, he thought, perpetually left behind, and sore. Veronica was ideally suited to the lower bureaucracy. He had almost dismissed her by the time he got to his room. He wanted to tell someone about the auction and boast about his prize. But Gail would be at her office, and Roger disliked bandying words with her secretary. There was something knowing about the woman—a hint of scorn or even ridicule. He suspected Gail of confiding in her. Some women banded together in a wearisome way, which in fact drove a man to rebel. The thin Santa Fe telephone book caught his eye, and to his surprise Sunny was listed.

If he seemed to have chosen the wrong fork, he would head for home, Roger told himself. After all, his employees had been unsupervised for a week now. But eventually the wheels struck the flat steel bars of a cattle guard, setting up a buzz that Roger felt in his bones and teeth.

"Turn right," he muttered.

The road angled between piñon pine and juniper trees, up into the hills. In places it was nearly washed out. He drove for two miles and noticed that the color of the mountains had thickened, and their nap of distant vegetation was now more perceptible. Time was passing.

What was the name of that pottery shop? "Feat of Clay"? Either that or some other specimen of hippie cuteness, he thought wryly. His own store was called simply Biscay's.

More than five years earlier, Roger had been walking past the open door when he heard the arresting sound of breaking dishes. Other decrescendos followed: peals of female laughter. In the gloomy, crowded shop he made out the figures of two young women. Veronica, on her hands and knees, was collecting shards of smashed pottery. Sunny stood over her, doubled up with amusement. Then she noticed Roger, and as she straightened her body he watched her loose breasts move beneath the thin fabric of her dress, like sleepers under the covers.

"May I help you?"

Roger hesitated. Sunny's laughter burst through her false solicitous tone and infected him, too.

Veronica called reproachfully from the back: "This one cost eighty dollars, Sunny."

"Well, it was ugly," Sunny said over her shoulder.

"Most of this stuff is ugly," said Roger, with a sense of brilliant discovery. "College-educated mud pies."

Sunny threw back her head in delight. He could still see that dress of hers, its long folds of Mexican cotton, faintly harsh and smelling of bread. It was embroidered in hot colors; tiny, crude human shapes peeped through twining vines. In the end they had left Veronica to tend the shop alone.

He gripped and released the steering wheel. The light had richened by another degree; his watch read three-fifteen. Another vehicle was approaching, an old pickup truck loaded with children and scavenged firewood. Roger waved, and the driver pulled over and waited in silence.

"I'm looking for a place." How could he seriously ask the way to a castle? The other man said nothing to help him, but the dark-eyed children let out a few titters.

"A big house, somewhere near," Roger finished lamely. He hated to ask directions, and children discomfited him. Recently Gail had begun to drop hints on this topic, but so far he'd ignored her.

"My father doesn't speak English." One of the passengers was a girl in her teens, with a shock of iridescent black hair. She reminded him of his first wife Isabel in high school, and he fended off a second memory of Isabel's face as he had last seen it, swollen by weeping.

The girl added, "There's a turnoff just ahead."

There he found a pair of adobe gateposts. Once thick but now half melted, they supported a curved dead bough forming a rough arch over the road. Two rusty chains dangled from the branch, but the sign that presumably once had hung there was gone. He eased the car around the rocks, feeling that he was near the end of his quest and that his logic was indisputable. Why not visit an old friend? As Gail herself would say, the simplest explanation made the best defense. She wasn't really a jealous woman. Roger reached a hilltop, and the trees fell away to reveal a building in the distance. It resembled a beached ark rather than a mansion. His heartbeat quickened.

He forded a sticky little stream; the water was deeper than he'd guessed. A dun-colored animal bolted across the road. A coyote? A fox? A dog? For now he came to a derelict gatehouse surrounded by patches of lawn. The road continued uphill, and in a moment he had reached the Castle.

Roger's first emotion was annoyance. His car was only the latest of many to arrive, and Sunny did not appear. The house was eccentric: modernist decks, railings, and funnels had been grafted onto an indigenous building. Roger saw a broken window on the second story. The metal pipes had bled freely down the faded pink stucco. A sprinkler described a watery cage on the front lawn, and smoke crept sideways behind it, pleasantly stinging Roger's nostrils and bringing a rush of saliva to his mouth. Something was cooking. Then he saw a naked blonde emerge from the front door, cross the lawn, and disappear into a clump of trees.

Had she overlooked him—or just ignored him? Automatically he followed her, pricked by thorns as he passed. Within a clearing he found a cement-sided pool half sunk in the ground, and not one but two blonde heads were floating in it.

"Hi," whispered one of them.

Smiling secretively, they contemplated him. An apparatus of wires and cables was strung above the tank; a broken trapeze had been tossed into the treetops.

A familiar voice penetrated the woods. "Roger! Are you there?"

One of the girls made a surface dive. Roger tried to pull his eyes away from the pulsating white limbs veiled with green water.

"Ah!" Sunny threw her arms around him. "You're still beautiful."

"You too."

He held her at arm's length. The same thick dark hair sheeted down her back; the irises of her eyes were mottled green and brown, amphibious; she wore a trailing dress.

"So fantastic!"

He could feel her warm skin through the sheer fabric as she drew him along the path.

"Your directions were terrible." As always, his desire was mixed with irritation.

"Poor Roger, did I lead you astray?" Sunny squeaked, without regret. "I've never driven it myself, you see."

A puff of smoke caught them full in the face.

"What's going on here?" Roger asked, coughing.

"We're roasting a pig."

"No, I mean this place. This house. You."

"I'm housesitting." Sunny traced a line in his forehead. "You always had the most beautiful eyebrows," she said.

The front door released a burst of people and noise from inside the house. Roger recognized an old Bob Dylan song:

*It ain't me you're looking for, babe.*
*Go melt back into the night.*
*Everything inside is made of stone.*
*There's nothing in here moving.*
*And anyway I'm not alone.*

The other guests were about Roger's age and slightly dilapidated. Dylan's nasal voice rang out as fresh as ever, but hairlines had eroded, waists thickened, clothes faded, and wire-rimmed glasses gone out of style. Roger thought of Southwestern cave mummies with fragments of cloth still clinging to their leather bodies. Chilled, he watched them wander off, some drinking from Styrofoam cups, some from crystal wine glasses. A whiff of marijuana remained behind them.

Sunny led him in another direction, through a crowded garage that smelled of tomcats and mice, past an old Mercedes up on blocks, and along a dark passage hung with hard and sharp objects.

"The kitchen is this way," she explained. "Oh, did you hurt your head? And besides, I didn't want to talk to the people in the living room."

"Who are they?"

"Oh, friends. Friends of friends." She held a door open. "Quick!"

Sudden light dazzled him, and he stumbled.

"The bird room," said Sunny. A sun porch had been fitted with flower beds and, oddly, a wall of bookcases. A few diseased geraniums were the only live plants left. A spasm ran through the stagnant air, smelling of ponds and mildewed paper; Roger rubbed his tingling earlobe. Sunny clapped her hands.

"Get away!" she cried. She dragged Roger through a second door and slammed it.

A note was taped to the glass: "Don't let birds out. Cats!"

"Luckily," Sunny said, "there's only like two canaries left."

Every flat surface in the kitchen overflowed with food or dirty dishes. Roger lifted an enormous loaf of bread from a stool and sat down.

"Want something to drink—or smoke?"

"Frankly, I'm starving. No lunch."

She laughed. "Good. Help yourself."

He ripped the end off the light log of bread.

"Try some hummus," she said. "I added a few mushrooms."

He rolled the grainy substance doubtfully over his tongue.

"Now tell me everything." Sunny dipped a grape in sour cream, then brown sugar.

"Everything?"

He felt the onset of thirst. On the floor by his feet stood several gallon jugs of wine and also a silver champagne cooler being used as a trash can.

"Well," he said. "I inherited the shop. My father died, so now I'm Biscay of Biscay's."

Biscay of Biscay's. A third generation Indian arts dealer. Several times lately he'd caught himself repeating those phrases.

"Still in Tucson?"

"Yes. Biscay's has changed a bit, though. I've put some capital into it, made it more of an art gallery, less of a curio shop. Big-ticket items give you higher profits."

"I get this craving for fruit," she said dreamily. "And are you still married?"

"Married again."

"I was married too. In the Native American Church. Well, Veronica probably told you. She never understood José at all."

"She's changed."

"Yes, she's a real little bureaucrat now." Sunny dabbed at a dribble of cream upon her bodice, which sparkled with silver bugle beads. "What does your wife do?"

"She's an attorney."

"Oh! Now your other wife—Isabel?—she was a schoolteacher, wasn't she?"

He agreed, remembering with a prickle of foreboding Sunny's shameless curiosity about Isabel.

"What's your new wife's name?"

"I went to an auction this morning in Santa Fe," Roger said. He described the McFarland sisters, whose extraordinary collection of Indian arts and crafts had been nearly unknown before the younger sister's recent death, at ninety-nine. Every wall and cupboard in their house was full of artifacts.

"What did you buy?"

"A Navajo rug. A beauty. Actually, it's out in the car."

"Oh, can I see it?"

A woman's voice called, "Sunny! Tyler says the pig is done."

She jumped up. "Later," she whispered. "I have to talk to you later."

Roger strayed into the living room, which was carpeted in white fur, none too clean. Seated around a brass coffee table, four men raised their heads as he passed; he saw that they were all Latins. On another table a large book lay open to a tinted engraving of a wild goose. The creature stood on a promontory, stretching its feathered serpent neck toward the waves that surrounded it on three sides. Roger turned to the title page: *The Birds of America* by John James Audubon, dated 1836. Excitedly he opened the next book on the table. It was a dogeared thriller ten years old. He dusted grit from his fingertips. Then he became aware of the pointed silence in the room behind him.

The pig had been roasted in a pit. The crowd scattered over the grass and decaying lawn furniture to eat in small separate groups; Roger found himself alone. He got the impression that this was an intertribal gathering: currents of discomfort flowed from group to group. He finally spotted one of the blondes, clothed and obviously accompanying a large bearded man in a black leather jacket. Sunny was eating with the man who had carved the pig, in swift strokes of a long blade like a machete or a sword. Roger swallowed the sweet smoky flesh. The jug wine, which smacked of kerosene, set up a kind of harmonic hum inside his head. The Latins perched gingerly along a low wall and spoke Spanish among themselves. A draft slid across the lawn with the dusk, stirring the bushes that swam in the high grass, and Roger caught the scent of fading roses and shivered.

Sunny wandered from group to group. When she bent over a frizzy-haired woman nursing a baby, Roger averted his eyes and saw that the man who had sliced the meat was watching Sunny too. At last she made a detour around the Latins and came to Roger.

"Tyler wants to meet you," she said, putting out a hand.

Roger stood up without touching her. Afterward he would seize the chance to leave, he thought. Tyler sat motionless. He was neither young nor middle-aged, a person of conventional appearance, the kind of man, Roger thought, who has sparse whiskers and a soft skin.

"So you're an old friend," Tyler said. His handshake was surprisingly painful. "Welcome to the Castle. Spending the night?"

"No," Roger answered quickly.

"But I haven't shown you the house yet," Sunny protested.

She captured his hand. Smiling faintly, Tyler strolled away; in a moment Roger heard him speaking Spanish.

"Why do you call it the Castle?"

"The owner does." Sunny danced ahead of him in slow circles that lifted the folds of her dress. The silver beads glittered like pins.

"Who is he?"

"She." Sunny touched a light switch in the foyer. "Look!"

The walls were covered with pictures of ocean liners. Then Roger saw that they all represented the same ship, and it was sinking.

"The *Titanic*?"

Sunny pointed at the ceiling. Ten feet above their heads a large fragment of some wooden structure dangled from chains.

"It's supposed to be part of a lifeboat," she said. "The man who built this house was like obsessed with the *Titanic*. He even named his daughter Titania. She owns the house now."

They moved into the deserted living room.

"There's a very valuable book over there," Roger said.

"Oh?"

A delicate scale and a plastic bag had been left behind upon the brass coffee table. He followed her up a circular staircase and through a labyrinth of halls lined with framed menus, passenger lists, dance programs, and shipwreck scenes.

"The queen of Santa Fe," said Sunny. "Titania calls herself the queen of Santa Fe. She's had four husbands. The first one hung himself, and she tore that part of the Castle down afterwards. Either the second or the third was a trapeze artist, and she rigged up the swimming pool for him to practice. It's fed by a spring up the hill. There used to be ducks in it, but they died."

"Where is she now?"

"Maine. She also owns an island in Maine. Her fourth husband hates this house. He's younger than Titania . . . some people call her the queen of the fairies. She telephones me all the time, late at night." Sunny pushed open a door. "This is my room. Titania's too."

The windows were blue-black; night had closed in. Little lamps dimly lit the huge bedroom. Mick Jagger grimaced down from a poster overlooking a shabby chintz chaise longue, a dressing table jammed with perfume bottles, and a round bed with an irregular brown and white cover. In front of the windows Roger saw the unexpected, homely shape of a sewing machine.

"Are you staying for the Opera?"

"No," he said. "I hate Sante Fe when it's full of tourists."

"I'm making some of the costumes."

She held up a mass of blue chiffon tentacles, then a German peasant dress. "Once I made a suit of chain mail."

"I didn't know you could sew."

"Oh, yes. That's how I met Titania. I made her a caftan, beaded like this."

Roger tried to imagine a domestic Sunny who calmly lifted her head from her sewing when he entered the room.

"In fact, this is hers. I borrowed it out of closet for the party," Sunny giggled.

"What are the operas?"

"*Manon*, I think. And a new one, like a premiere, called *Lorenzo in Taos*—about D. H. Lawrence."

"You know," said Roger, "the McFarland sisters, the ones with the rug, could even have met him."

"Fantastic," said Sunny. She lit a candle at the dressing table. "People were more real back then."

Roger placed his hands on her shoulders. They were plump and firm, unlike his wife Gail's which were sharp with bones.

"You feel real enough to me," he said.

Within the crystal flasks the perfumes had shrunk into yellow stains. Lined up in front of them were a black pebble, a peacock feather, a cowrie shell, and a shred of snakeskin: the fetishes of a child or a shaman. The cheap white candle was thrust into an empty bottle labeled Château d'Yquem. He remembered Sunny's fondness for fire. A small flame always used to flutter beside her bed, casting confused shadows upon the wall, and sure enough now he saw another candle sprouting from a Chablis jug by the circular bed. They moved toward it. The bedspread changed into something hairy, monstrous.

"My God! What's that?"

"A Hereford cowhide."

He took an involuntary step backward, crushing some fragile object beneath his heel. He stepped again and apparently landed upon several tiny rollers.

"What's so funny?" Roger snapped.

"It's just a graham cracker."

The floor was sprinkled with crumbs and wooden matches, some new and some spent. As he stared at them he heard first the muffled throb of drums from the party below and then a clatter on the roof, too loud for rats or squirrels.

"Dogs," explained Sunny, convulsed again. "The house is built into the hillside, and dogs run onto the roof. They wake us up in the morning."

Roger said that he must go.

"No!" She followed him down the hall.

"Why not?" he asked grudgingly, but already his anger and disgust were lessening.

"Go get your Navajo rug," Sunny whispered. "You can show it to me. Nobody will think anything, and we can talk. Please. It's important."

"You're in some kind of trouble," he said.

She brushed ahead of him and down the twisting stairs. In the living room two women were dancing slowly together, their arms waving like loose tissue underwater.

Roger located his car among the new Jeeps and vans in the driveway, and as he opened the door a wave of fear hit him: he'd forgotten to lock it up. He cursed and fumbled until he touched wool. The rug was still there. And after all, were these people likely to know its value? A few silhouettes stood out against the orange coals of the barbecue pit; one of them might be Tyler. It would be easy, Roger thought, to drive away, just as he had done five years ago. But as he hesitated a female figure drifted up to the front window and stood there alone, and Roger moved toward the light.

"What did you put in the coffee?"

"Only cardomom. That's how they drink it in Israel. I lived on a kibbutz once, you know."

"You?"

"I had a boyfriend. . . . It was a long time ago."

At this altitude the coffee steamed abundantly but it was not very hot.

Roger said, "What's the matter?"

"Quick, unroll the rug," she breathed. Then her voice soared and cracked. "Tyler! See what Roger brought?"

The rug looked even better than Roger had remembered. Into the small dark den where she had led them it introduced a fourth presence, a spirit firmly balanced, intricate, and bold.

"Roger's like an Indian trader," Sunny said. "Isn't this fantastic? I love Granada red."

"Ganado red," Roger muttered.

"Garish, isn't it?" Tyler said at last. He was still wearing a small smile.

"No, look how it suits this room. He got it from a little old lady who knew D. H. Lawrence."

"I guess if I buy the house I'll need a few more things. It's been stripped of the good stuff." Tyler turned to Roger. "How much do you want for it? I may buy the house."

He tossed out words like a man flicking trash into water. Roger felt himself stiffening.

"I'm not sure," he said. "It's antique, it's big, and it's in perfect condition. I don't think it's ever been on the floor."

"Come on, man," Tyler said. "Just double what you paid for it, right?"

"That may not be enough."

"No good deals for old friends?" Tyler jeered.

"It's rare. Maybe museum quality. I should do some research before I price it."

Roger ran his hand over the taut weaving, passing from clear scarlet to white to gray to black. Suddenly he saw himself at work in his office at Biscay's. Shafts of sunlight penetrated the burglar bars across the window and branded his papers bright and dark. Instrument of pure truth and pleasant deams, his calculator lay at his right hand. He was looking forward to buying a computer when he got home. Perhaps he would keep this rug for himself after all.

"Five thousand," he said.

Tyler snorted. "If he decides to sell it," he told Sunny, "you can pay fifteen hundred. I'm taking Pepe and Genaro and the others to the plane."

Fifteen hundred dollars was precisely the bargain bid that Roger had made that morning. He turned away to hide his uneasiness, and Tyler banged the door shut.

"Tyler's going all the way to Albuquerque, this late?"

"No," said Sunny. She knelt at the beehive fireplace and struck a match. "There's an airstrip on the mesa."

"What does Tyler do, anyway?"

She hesitated. "He's like a broker. From here to Latin America."

"Brokering what?"

She paused again. "He supplies the freedom fighters," she said finally.

"That was freedom they were weighing on the coffee table?"

"He sends guns to the freedom fighters!"

"Will he really buy this house?"

"He made an offer," Sunny said sulkily, "but Titania said it was too low."

"And you want to leave him?" She wasn't a prisoner, Roger pointed out. There was a telephone in the kitchen, surrounded by names and numbers scrawled directly on the wall.

"I don't have a car," she said in a smothered voice. "He drives me. And Roger, I loved you."

"Loved." He repeated the sound of an object sliding, then stopping with a thud. "Why did you do what you did? Isabel— "

"I just thought she should know the truth."

He laughed sharply. "So tell it to Tyler."

"Oh, why did you even come?" Sunny let herself collapse on the rug.

"I don't know," said Roger. "I don't even know your real name."

He looked at the short, curved hairs on the exposed nape of her neck. Slowly she stretched herself out under his gaze until she lay at full length, propped on one elbow. Behind her the fire shot its red, yellow, and blue plumage upward, and Sunny's dress shimmered like the skin of a fish. He wondered why the fabric was wet all around the hem.

"My name is Mary Malinowsky. My father's in the insurance business in Omaha. My mother's a housewife. I'm thirty-four."

Her hair was warm next to the scalp, then cool and tangled. Moved, Roger discovered new white hairs writhing beneath the dark ones over her temple.

"Roger," she said, "when the sun is bright, you know how you can see like little specks in the air? Just floating around?"

"Dust," he said, swallowing. "Why?"

He touched the beadwork on her chest; he stroked his palm across dozens of tiny snags. She laughed, and at this distance he could hear the full texture of it, each squeak and gurgle in her throat. She smelled of musk and roasted meat.

"Because that's all there is to it, really. I figured it out. Just little dots. Everywhere."

Roger was barely listening. The fire gave off a sent of incense. His hand traveled past her ribs and stopped short. Sunny was getting fat, he thought. The voluminous dress concealed a bulge of flesh above the pubic bone: odd, misplaced almost. He sat up.

"Sunny."

The face was foreign to him. Puckered and watchful, it seemed to be holding its breath, and he knew that what he suspected was true.

"What are you going to do?" Roger asked formally.

She lay quiet. A log snapped in the fireplace and sent sparks sizzling over the hearth.

"The rug! Get up!"

He dragged the rug out from under her, flapped it, anxiously searched it for damage. Sunny shook out her skirts. At her bare feet a small coal cooled from red to black upon the wooden floor.

"How can you burn juniper without a fire screen?"

"It smells good. Don't put me down," she said loudly.

He started to roll up the rug, which was apparently unscorched. "So you won't take me?"

Standing over him Sunny seemed enormous, already swollen by pregnancy. Her gray hair showed. Roger rose appalled, with the woolen cylinder drooping over his shoulder. It was worth three thousand at least, he told himself, and he thought of his shop again. When Isabel had divorced him, there was little property to divide; besides, Isabel was a weeper, not a fighter. Now he owned Biscay's. Or did he? Gail had begun by lending him money, but their current finances were fully entangled. Roger remembered the way she clicked her polished fingernails against the desk as she examined the books of the business. Bankruptcy was her specialty, but she could also triumph in divorce. In fact, Roger thought she would pick him clean.

"Sunny," he said, "are you crazy? Or just stupid?"

The coffee cup spun past his head and shattered against the doorjamb. At his back he heard Sunny's laughter, shrill now. He kept on walking. Yellowed, cracked life preservers protruded from the walls. He crossed the living room in the role of nonchalant departing guest. The man in the black leather jacket sat on the sofa, each arm draped around a blonde; Roger saw that he wore a small Yale padlock through one earlobe.

Outside, Roger clasped the rug in his arms and allowed himself to run. At the last moment he evaded the sprinkler. There was no sign of Tyler. He gunned the engine and bumped down the hill into the dark. Spurting ahead of him, the headlights revealed tumbling galaxies of dust. The particles marked their courses, plunged, and disappeared almost as fast as he saw them.

At the vista point where he had stopped earlier, Roger looked back. Juniper smoke still tingled in his nose. Clouds had lowered the sky; the world was nearly blacked out. But colored light spilled from the Castle, which lay askew on its hilltop like a listing, burning ship. Roger tasted the initial awe, the selfish joy, and the shame of a refugee. These faded, and he drove on.

IV

# *The Glass House*

## 1980

Lewis March raised the crowbar in both hands and rammed it into the ground. Each buried blow made a sound like a cough. As he was shoveling smashed chalky rock and dirt from the hole, a woman drove up in a small yellow pickup truck.

Sweating hard, Lewis leaned on his shovel and watched her carry a toolbox into the unfinished house. Then she returned to her truck and dragged out a long flat object sheathed in cardboard.

"Need some help?"

"No."

He hurried to open the door anyway. She did not thank him.

"I made it," she said. "I'm used to moving it around."

The door swung shut, and they stood together in a pile of sawdust. Even in the full blaze of an Arizona June, the aroma called up phantom forests, dark and perpendicular in his mind. "What is that?" Lewis asked.

"A stained glass window," she said grudgingly.

She unpacked a hammer, a screwdriver, and a wrench. When she removed the cardboard he said, with a touch of irony: "Ah, little desert animals."

A rabbit, a quail, a roadrunner, a lizard, and a snake chased one another across the window.

"It's not my taste," she flashed. "I needed the commission."

"Nice, but the ears are wrong," Lewis said pointing at the rabbit. "Looks like an Eastern cottontail, not Arizonan."

"And who are you?"

Lewis looked down at his threadbare Levi's, his hands and feet caked with dirt, and his bare chest, burned past tan to ashy black. His gut at thirty-six was only slightly soft. She was about his own age, he estimated. Cropped hair seemed to grip her skull with tiny paws; brown and gray clothes hung from a thin body. Everything about her, including the tools, was scrupulously clean.

"I majored in biology," he said mildly.

"Oh?"

"Now I'm a landscaper. I needed a job too."

As she turned her back he noticed that she wore a yellow metal belt elaborately decorated with bosses, studs, and little spikes.

Lewis came late to the opening, but he found the shabby gallery crowded. Free beer still flowed, attracting ragged street people as well as members and friends of the Tucson Artists' Collective. Beneath a skin of new paint, the building, a former shoe store, was slowly falling down. Lewis nodded to an acquaintance who dealt in Navajo rugs, to a pigtailed rock musician, and to an old girl friend. When he had recovered from the slight jolt of seeing her again, he worked his way down the room. Since the floorboards had both warped and settled, this was a matter of following the grade. He spotted his neighbor Tom Kaplan, who had a painting on display. "Surrounded by women, as usual," Lewis said to himself. As he joined the group, a chin lifted, and Lewis found himself face to face with the woman who made stained glass.

Tom's erotic antennae quivered visibly. "You two know each other?"

"No," she said.

"We've met," Lewis said simultaneously.

Tom grinned. "Barbara Dominick, Lewis March. Barbara has a piece of stained glass in the show. Lewis runs a landscaping business."

"We're working on the same house," she said at last.

Lewis noticed that her upper lip was deeply and curiously cleft at the center.

"Will you show me your work?"

Suspended on nearly invisible fish line, the panel was abstract and colorless.

"I like beveled glass," Lewis said cautiously.

Barbara was silent.

"So this is more your taste?" he went on. "I did appreciate the other one, too."

"Those people," she said, "can buy what they like."

"Yeah. Their landscaping is supposed to cost one quarter of the value of the house, and to take care of itself. Beyond that, they're not interested."

She stared at the glass panel. "Ice," he thought. "A design in ice."

A tramp sloshing a plastic cup of beer came staggering between them and the glass. His bedroll was slung across his back, and he traveled with dilated eyes through an alien country. The glass panel swayed. Lewis took a step forward, but Barbara touched his arm.

"No," she said.

The crowd parted to let the transient pass. In their faces Lewis recognized pity, disgust, indecision, and fear. The man reached the door and plunged into the hot night; Lewis turned to Barbara. "Why, she looks friendly," Lewis thought. The expression of camaraderie faded from her face. Now Lewis saw what she thought of *him*: a thick figure blocking the light. On his arm the place where she had laid her finger stung.

"The Glass House," Lewis read. He traced the words in the telephone book: "Stained. Beveled. Etched. Custom windows, lamps. Repairs and restoration. Classes. Barbara Dominick."

The voice on the answering machine seemed to speak from the far end of a tunnel. "This is the Glass House," it said. If he left his name and number, she would return his call.

But she did not.

One day after work Lewis dropped by to see Tom, who lived in an Art Deco filling station down the block and painted in the former garage. A petroleum tang lingered beneath the smell of acrylic paint; spatters of Da-Glo orange and green half hid the grease stains. But Lewis saw that Tom had entered a new phase. He hung sideways from a ladder, painting the top of a giant canvas battleship gray.

"They're getting bigger," Lewis observed.

Tom grunted.

Lewis propped a three-legged chair against the wall and straddled it quietly until Tom came down.

"Only museum walls are big enough," Tom boasted. "I'm building up inventory. How are you?"

Lewis said, "Tell me about Barbara Dominick."

Tom laughed and shook his head. "So that's it. I've never had any luck with that chick. You're setting yourself up for one of your tragedies."

Women passed continually through the filling station, but Tom's amiable egotism never wavered. He was not, Lewis thought, really susceptible to passion.

"Her stuff is good," said Tom. "If you like stained glass."

"Is she single?"

"Very!"

Lewis decided to take a class. She could hardly refuse him that, he guessed. Yet as he searched for the Glass House on the first evening he was feeling both righteous and sly.

It was a neighborhood of small irregular buildings, a place where scissors might be ground and poodles groomed. He drove past green gravel lawns, homemade wishing wells, and converted school buses up on blocks. A high fence hid Barbara's house from the street. Lewis prodded at the gate, which finally yielded to his shoulder. He fell into her garden. Old entangled trees made it dim. Regaining his balance, he identified the scents of pepper, cypress, and pine. Wet grass pricked his feet through his track shoes. The place seemed deserted, and he wondered if he had come on the wrong night.

A trace of exotic perfume drifted by. It was tantalizingly familiar, and he looked up and down for its source. What woman in his past had worn it? Suddenly he saw a white water lily apparently floating vertically in the hot dusky air.

"Night-blooming cereus."

Speaking his thoughts aloud, the voice sprang from a point close to his ear. He spun around and confronted her. Her clothes blended into the dark: only a pale face and long bare arms were visible, and then, as she moved, a pearly starfish pendant swung away from her chest. Lewis tried to force his heart to slow down.

"Strange cactus," he said. "Looks like a dry stick most of the year."

"Not now."

"Even when it seems dead, there's that huge tuber below ground. They must taste good. My dog tries to dig them up and eat them."

"I have cats."

Lewis leaned over the flower.

"Up close," Barbara said, "it's too sweet."

Lewis started to laugh. "It has thorns, too."

"The class is in the studio at the back," she said stiffly.

The only man among five women, he arranged himself in a humble position to receive information. The women had brought notebooks. The first session was to be a lecture and demonstration, it appeared.

The studio was a separate building from her house. It contained three high work tables, various racks of equipment, and a row of storage bins for glass. Lewis idly pulled out a crimson pane. Barbara stopped in midsentence.

"It's sharp."

"Sorry."

Chartres. Burne-Jones. The arts and crafts movement. Tiffany glass. Chagall. Lewis, who regularly got up at four in the morning, fell into a pleasant stupor. He watched her mouth move as she spoke a fanciful language: horseshoe nails, lead leaf, lathekins, roundels, liver of sulfur, patinas, grozing. At last she held up a small tool and he caught the word "diamonds." The women all stood up for the demonstration, and Lewis hauled himself into the back row. His head cleared. He wondered why on a summer evening she was dressed in black.

She scored a sheet of greenish glass. Then she tapped steadily along the groove; the glass dropped in two; the audience exhaled. Barbara smiled, but Lewis almost thought she was disappointed.

"Sometimes it fails," she said.

Noticing several finished panels stacked against the wall, Lewis hung back as the other students left. The first design reminded him of blue and purple canyons, while the second was a conventional floral piece. The third shocked him. In hot colors and broken shapes, it showed a woman being demolished by a huge car. Her legs were splayed suggestively in a pool of blood. Her mouth screamed.

"What are you doing?"

He dropped the panel, and she let out a cry. They scrabbled on the floor together.

"I'm sorry. I'm really sorry. I don't think it's broken."

"Never mind. Why are you harassing me?"

"If I've broken something, I'll buy it."

"I don't care if it breaks. I like it to break. Why can't you leave me alone? Why me?"

"You fascinate me."

"It's unintentional. You slept during class."

"I did not," he said, and quoted: " 'Keep a good edge on your knife. You don't want to crush the heart of the lead.' "

Barbara hid the panel again behind the others.

"I'm not an artist," Lewis said. "You're right about that. I just plant plants. I have friends who are, though, and I admire it. I have my nose against the window."

This time he could not read her mind at all. The long, dented mouth twisted, and at last she said: "Stained glass is not art."

"Why not?"

"It's decoration. A craft. A typical women's hobby. And this town is a backwater. At least," she said bitterly, "plants grow."

"Not necessarily," Lewis said. "Good or not, you have to take satisfaction in what you do." He drew in a long breath. "Or make a change."

They were still sitting on the floor in a kind of intimacy. He hoped she might offer a reason to stay longer, but she rose without doing so.

"So how's it going?" asked Tom.

"I'm making a window," Lewis said.

Each leaned his back against an antique gasoline pump like a crude cologne atomizer. They watched the July sun drop behind a mass of clouds and emerge just above the horizon: a red muffled gong.

"What does that mean?"

"There's an ex-husband in the picture. Old bad vibes."

Tom shook his head. "I'm not an animal trainer myself," he said complacently.

Lewis amused himself by picturing Tom, hair bleached, spangles pasted to his chest, dangling a thin lash; a drove of nude women lumbered around a ring.

"I think Carolyn set out some sun tea before she went to work," Tom said. "Or there's beer."

Lewis could see a bottle of black tea at the edge of the sidewalk.

"You need some shade out here," he said. "Tell you what. You know that painting I like? The one that looks like chicken feet? I'll trade you a couple of mesquite trees for it."

"What kind of mesquite?" Tom asked suspiciously.

"Argentine. They're fast growing. Next summer, if you water them enough, you'll have shade."

"Maybe you could keep an eye on them for me," Tom said.

Lewis had persuaded Barbara to eat a meal with him. But when he mentioned a restaurant she declared that she would meet him there.

"I'll pick you up."

"No need."

He thought for a moment.

"I know," he said. "You pick me up."

"Why?"

"I'll show you where my window will go."

"If you ever finish it."

As the time approached, he went again and again to the peephole in his front door. He could not quite believe that she would come, but at last she stood on the step, wearing one of her drooping dresses and a silver necklace like a shackle. Her eyes skimmed over the arrangement of objects in the room: colored shapes, easy chairs, green leaves. He knew enough of Barbara now to interpret her look of glittering scorn as fear.

"One of Tom's?" she asked, focusing on a painting.

"Yes. It's new."

His old golden retriever sniffed at Barbara's ankles and subsided into sleep again.

"You collect," she said accusingly.

"Not really," Lewis said. "I like Navajo rugs, especially old ones."

He showed her a square chief's blanket woven in stripes of indigo and yellowed white wool, and then a Germantown "eye-dazzler" made up of zigzag puzzle pieces in fiery aniline colors.

"They're beautiful," Barbara said in a low voice.

"Well, they're faded old rugs. The wool has a kind of life to it, though, and you can actually use a rug. More than a piece of canvas smeared with acrylic paint."

"Or glass?" She fingered the silver band around her throat.

"Windows are basic," Lewis said, turning his key in the lock. "So is decoration. Isn't it?"

He was relieved when she ordered a full meal and ate it greedily. Finishing first, Barbara caught him staring.

"What is it?" she snapped.

"I thought you might be a vegetarian."

The viscous red wine had altered both of them. She crowed with laughter, and he, annoyed, made a row of creases in the tablecloth with his fork. She unbuckled her choker, pushed her sleeves, and said, "Let's have dessert."

Pink stucco was dropping from her house in chunks, like frosting from dark dry cake. A cactus hedge partly concealed the dilapidation, but as he stepped inside, Lewis found himself recalling the name of a plasterer. He could make a deal with Oscar . . . and then he suppressed the thought as premature.

The rooms were nearly empty. All walls were white, and the furniture was made of reeds and straw. Barbara measured coffee; Lewis leaned against a bulbous old refrigerator. Through the open bedroom door he saw a single bed.

"Where's the stained glass?" he asked.

"There's a window in the living room. One piece is plenty for a house."

"You're not much of an advertiser," he teased.

Flames leaped up under the coffee pot, but Barbara said nothing.

"Why," said Lewis, "did you say that you liked glass to break?"

The coffee smoked in thick mugs.

"Do you have any sugar?"

She turned to him at this and answered seriously: "It's a thing, just a thing. They weigh me down."

"Well, I guess I can drink it black."

She burst out laughing. "I mean glass! When glass breaks I just sweep it away. Clean."

She pushed a small bowl of sugar toward him.

"Then what?" Lewis asked, stirring.

"I start over. But I'm never satisfied."

"It's a thrill, too. Isn't it?"

"What?"

"Breaking glass."

She looked startled.

"That was very good coffee," Lewis said.

"Thanks. It's time for you to go now," Barbara said abruptly.

When they passed across the moonlit lawn Lewis noticed that the night-blooming cereus had produced a single spiny fruit, now half devoured by birds.

Barbara had tapped and wedged a mosaic of cobalt blue and copper colored lozenges between bands of lead. She started to solder the joints.

"Shouldn't you wear a mask?" Lewis asked.

"Why?"

He said something about lead fumes, which she shrugged off, moving the soldering iron quickly from point to point. Outside, the light faded suddenly, and the windows rattled and hissed. A sandstorm had hit the studio. Lewis saw the old trees rock energetically.

"It's going to rain," he remarked.

An orange flash dazzled their eyes. Half a second later, the bang came. Barbara gasped, and the studio lights went out.

"Unplug that thing," called Lewis, stumbling across the studio.

Rain sheeted down the windows, and a gale swallowed the Glass House, testing every frail element in the building. Lewis imagined the roof rafting on its own through the storm. They heard a siren at a great distance.

"I'll have to stay here till this lets up," Lewis said, thinking aloud.

Then he felt Barbara's fingers curl around his arm.

"At first I thought you were like Tom."

"I am like Tom."

And he tumbled off the narrow causeway that he had followed for three months: down, stripped, through thorns and abrasions to delicious slime.

Autumn always uplifted him. With the first break in the heat Lewis took new heart; it was a second spring. Whistling a song from high school, he stepped around a broken beer bottle upon the sidewalk and stopped short. A derelict unfolded himself from a squat against the nearest wall.

Younger than Lewis, able-bodied, he stretched out a hand tipped by broad, startlingly pale fingernails: "Spare change?"

In his September mood Lewis discovered a crumpled dollar bill in his pocket and passed it over.

"Get the hell off my property!"

A third man glared through the wrought iron that barred a high window. Beside it iron letters spelled out "Biscay's Indian Arts" against a white plaster wall.

"Not you, Lewis," he added.

A handful of brass bells hung from the back of the door, which Roger Biscay slammed after a last glance down the street.

"Those bums are ruining my business," he said. "They stink up the street, they hassle my customers—what did he say to you?"

Lewis thought of Roger's idealistic stint as a Vista volunteer years ago. He said, "Well, I gave him a buck."

"We may have to move. After fifty years in this shop, too." Roger told him rather sharply.

It was a Sonoran style row house probably dating from Territorial days. Under its cactus rib ceilings Roger sold silver and turquoise jewelry, sand paintings, Hopi kachinas, Seri wood carvings, fragrant green baskets, and round pots decorated with angular designs. Sometimes there was a Navajo woman weaving in a corner. The faintly meaty scent of new leather filled the moccasin section, where a shoemaker worked. Roger took advantage of his black hair and cultivated an Indian appearance himself.

"Tom says you've been dallying with stained glass," Roger went on.

"I still like rugs," Lewis returned, smiling.

"I got something in Santa Fe that might interest you."

They went into the rug room, and Roger searched through a pile of folded Navajo blankets. The larger ones thudded like falling bodies as he tossed them aside, gray, green, brown, and black.

"There. Look at that."

It was big, about six by nine feet, and patterned with black, gray, and white triangles. It was firm and silky, in prime condition, and in spite of the pattern of triangles it was fundamentally, unequivocally red. Lewis knew that he was lost.

"I wanted to keep this one," Roger said regretfully. "But Gail didn't like it. She's done the house in earth tones, and it didn't fit."

"It's a natural color," said Lewis. "Blood."

"It's a classic Ganado red. Commercial dye, of course. I date it about 1925."

As though indifferently, Lewis turned over a corner of the rug and read the price tag: $3500. He smoothed the corner back in place. Slowly he paced the full length of the rug, studying the symmetry of the design, the evenness of the dye, the quality of the warp and woof threads, and the neatness of the finishing details.

"I don't think it's ever been used," said Roger. "I bought it from the estate of two little old ladies in Santa Fe. This rug came out of a closet of brand new shoes and clothes from the Twenties—never been worn."

Lewis said nothing.

"Or I have a real pretty Teec Nos Pos rug. I know you don't like Two Gray Hills."

Lewis thought of lying on the rug, sinking into the scarlet core.

"I don't need to trade for landscaping right now, Lewis, but for an old friend I'd knock something off the price."

"I can pay," Lewis answered.

"What's that?" Barbara said, opening the door a crack.

"Aren't you going to let me in?"

The bundle was as long as a man and nearly as thick. Lewis laid it at one end of Barbara's living room floor and unrolled the big red rug.

"Like it?"

She took a step backward.

"It's an old Ganado red. I thought it would just fit here."

She covered her eyes. "No."

"Marry me."

"Trade one pain for another?"

"What about pleasure?"

She turned away. He smelled the lanolin in the wool, felt its fibers tickling his skin through his clothes. Sunlight of a September richness made the rug bloom. Through the window he glimpsed a row of sparrows poised along a wire like a sequence of musical notes.

She said, "You have a house."

"I'll rent it."

"The dog—the cats."

"They'll work it out."

"Or eat each other up."

At last she examined the rug, saying in a trembling voice: "It builds up to the center, then breaks down."

"The design? Now, I'd say it builds from both ends and meets in the middle. It's not so tragic."

The perimeter of the windowpane was beveled. Lewis watched the sparrows as one by one they swelled, wavered, and darted beyond his vision, their drab feathers edged with watery rainbows.

"Marry me," he repeated. "Marry me. Marry me. Marry me."

V

# *The Lighthouse Keeper*

1981

Barbara Dominick held a blue glass disk before her eyes.

Tucson, Arizona turned into Antarctica. Her room sank under icy water, and the red Navajo rug darkened to wine color.

Even after many years of working with glass, she still enjoyed this game. She chose a ruby disk, looked again, and caught her breath. The rug was now dead gray with a spiked black pattern. A pink cat minced across it, followed by a pair of brown boots.

"I didn't hear you come in," she said defensively.

"You gave me a key when you married me. Remember?"

Barbara whisked away the glass.

"What's that?" Lewis asked.

"The sun."

He sat down beside her: the wicker sofa creaked and wobbled. Barbara braced herself against the same tendency that overcame her in bed: rolling downhill to him. "A bride at thirty-six," she thought. "Exposed. Ridiculous." She pulled a lumpy piece of opalescent glass from beneath his thigh.

"And the moon," she said, making a mask of it.

Lewis lifted the glass away. "Handmade, isn't it? Expensive?"

"Married people always talk about money."

"Everybody talks about money, Barb," said Lewis equably.

She had never had a nickname before. Her first husband always said "you."

"You've got your business and I've got mine," Lewis said, stretching till his shoulders cracked. "I'll never get rich a-diggin' a ditch." He spread out his hands, and the ingrained dirt in his skin provoked her and melted her.

"Why do you still do it?" she asked.

"One of my laborers didn't show up."

"Fire him."

All the lines in Lewis's face tightened for an instant.

It was a mistake. Antarctica again, she thought. Why had he insisted on marrying her? He couldn't have understood that compared to him she was clever and bad. When he did, he would surely leave her, too.

"I never fired anybody in my life," she said quickly.

Lewis laughed. "Nobody could work for you. Listen, here's an aptitude test. Which would you choose to be, a headwaiter or a lighthouse keeper?"

She answered warily: "A lighthouse must be peaceful."

"I knew it!"

"But a headwaiter is the opposite of a desert landscaper."

"Well," he said, "wouldn't you get lonely in that lighthouse?"

"Just me, the light, and the sea. Simple. Clear."

"You had things pretty spare and bare before I came along, didn't you?" said Lewis, pulling her down onto the rug with him. "Do you regret this?"

So that she could keep her stained glass studio in the back yard, he had left his house for hers. But the paintings on the walls, once blank, had belonged to him. The large red rug was his wedding present to her. A king-size bed filled most of her small bedroom. She was blockaded, crushed, in bliss.

Triangles of black, gray, and white throbbed against the red wool beneath Lewis's shoulder. Barbara fixed her eyes on a single row of weaving and followed it to the black border of the rug.

"I got a big commission today." She smoothed her hair, shrinking from Lewis's enthusiasm. "A whole chapel for some nuns."

"Chapel! Saints and crosses?"

"Why not?"

"I guess I can't quite see you working for nuns."

"The theme is times of day. Suns and moons, remember?"

"Great." Lewis balanced the opal disk on the palm of one hand.

"In fact," Barbara said, "I know all about nuns."

The cat leaped into Lewis's lap and crooked her tail under his nose.

"I wish I could do something weightless—spaceless," Barbara burst out. "Something that wasn't clutter."

"But then it wouldn't exist," he said.

"A dance?"

"Dancers take up a lot of space."

"Music?"

"Ouch."

She aimed a punch at him. "Philosophy. Meditation."

"Let's have a burrito," Lewis suggested.

The chapel was hardly more than another waiting room in the nuns' hospital; they had decided to replace its five plain windows with stained glass. Barbara assembled the panels in chronological order, beginning with sunrise. Working with glass she was always happy, although she didn't realize it. It pleased her to think of the material as a supercooled fluid, not a solid. Even the vocabulary appealed to a hunger for richness that she usually denied in the rest of her life.

"Aventurine panels," she would say alone in her studio. "Millefiori. A streaky rondel, like an all-day sucker."

She laid down pieces of pale blue flashed with white: sky. She dressed the human figures in burnt orange and shocking pink, which she would never have worn herself. From the spiny branches of a malachite tree she hung purple apples. She had reached the middle of the night scene with its opal moon when she came home one afternoon and found her front door hanging open.

Lewis's dog stood in the hall and moved his tail tentatively. At first she thought Lewis was home early, but then she saw that every container in the house had been dumped.

A noise came from the kitchen. Fear took her breath away. Tracking flour, the cat appeared, and the fear turned to rage.

"Get out of here before I kill you!" she shouted into the house.

The cat rocketed past her and disappeared.

"Sorry," she said to the dog.

She plowed over to the telephone. "This is me, Barbara, calling the cops," she thought in disbelief. The voice at the other end was hardened: an officer would respond, and meanwhile nothing should be touched. The refrigerator hung open and the beer was gone. Barbara banged the door shut with her fist. In the bedroom she saw that her jewelry box was empty, the bed was torn apart, and Lewis's clothes were tangled up with hers on the floor.

She wandered back into the living room. Her undersized black and white television set was still there, but Lewis's stereo was not. The paintings lay on their faces. A cactus had been tipped from its pot, and beside it she noticed a spot of blood on the floor.

"Good," she muttered.

Then she realized that the floor was bare, the way it used to be. The Navajo rug was gone.

Lewis arrived at the same time as the police car.

"The rug," she called to him across the lawn. The heavy-footed men seemed to take hours to reach her.

"Cool down, Barb," Lewis said.

Impassively, without exerting himself, the policeman went through the house.

"What about the studio?" asked Lewis.

"Oh my God, I forgot. But there's nothing there to steal."

Even the policeman was startled by the drifts of broken glass they found.

"Vandalism." He shook his head. "Well, your average burglar is eighteen years old."

Lewis put his arm around Barbara's stiff shoulders and said something about insurance, but she twitched away.

"I'm not insured for this."

She began to make her way across the rubble.

"Be careful," Lewis said.

Ignoring him, she took inventory. The chapel windows were all broken, along with most of her supply of glass. There was, however, a heavy trail of blood throughout the studio, and a gory towel had been abandoned beneath a bush outside.

"I hope he bleeds to death," said Barbara intensely. She imagined jumping up and down on the body. "Are you going to check the hospitals?"

The officer looked up in surprise. "For a minor burglary?"

If there were a good chance of catching the thief, he said, that might be different.

"I've never been robbed before," said Barbara. "This is minor?"

"Burglarized," he corrected. "Yes, ma'am."

Lewis pointed out that the rug was worth as much as a used car.

"Thirty-five hundred, Mr. March. I got it down. My advice to you is to check the swap meets for a while. Sometimes you get lucky."

"We have a photograph of the rug," Lewis said.

"We'll put it in your file," the policeman promised, without enthusiasm.

When he and the fingerprint team were gone, Lewis and Barbara faced each other.

"Well, it's just things." Lewis tried again to touch her. "I thought you didn't like things."

"It's evil," she said angrily, her eyes on the empty place on the floor. Except for the paintings, the room now looked as it had when she lived alone. "I hope he gets infected and dies of a lingering disease."

She saw that Lewis was dismayed.

"Monster in full view," she thought in dark satisfaction.

"Never mind," Lewis murmured after a moment. "We're safe, anyhow."

She thought, "Are we?"

Twilight had drained the warmth from her surroundings and turned him into a shadow across the room.

"We'll replace the rug," he said. "It was insured."

"You told me each one is unique."

"Yes. Well, maybe I imposed that rug on you anyway. Maybe this time you'll let me give you a ring."

"I don't want a ring," Barbara said.

"Okay." Lewis switched on a light, paining her eyes. "Tomorrow I'll help you sweep out the studio. I'm very sorry about your windows."

"I can fix *that*."

His patience—or dullness—was ostentatious, she thought; she had never seen it fail him yet. They worked in silence among the ruins of their bedroom.

"Bad luck," said Roger Biscay pleasantly. "Sure, I'll update your appraisal."

Barbara plunged her fingers through a bowl of the polished obsidian pebbles called Apache tears. Male beauty rarely interested her, but the look in Roger's slowly rising eyes was somehow tantalizing. Had Lewis noticed? Perhaps Roger did it automatically, but she believed that a man like him did not usually make any effort at all, except to brush women off. She touched an icy silver bracelet, then the blue velvet blouse of an Indian doll. Its hair was surprisingly harsh. Roger's hair, she thought, would be silky. Lewis slumped beside him, dusty as always.

"How can we get it back?" she asked.

Roger shrugged. "Most likely it's already left southern Arizona," he said. "Stolen Indian artifacts are going to Europe these days, or to New York, or L.A."

"We have a picture," Barbara said.

"I could circulate copies to my dealers. You might send some out, too, although it's a long shot."

"Lewis just wants to get another rug," she said. "But I'm angry."

"I have a real pretty Teec Nos Pos rug," Roger said. "Unfortunately, antique Ganado reds like the one you lost don't turn up often."

"You said you bought it in Santa Fe," Lewis put in.

"Yes." An odd expression crossed Roger's face; almost alarm, Barbara thought, smoothed away quickly. "An old lady had died—very old, nearly a hundred—and left it unused in a closet, with lots of shoes, never worn. I went to an auction in the house. She and her sister lived there for sixty years, and actually they're buried in a huge marble tomb in the garden. The older sister died first."

"Weird for the younger one," said Lewis. "To live there alone, with her sister in the garden."

"Maybe it was a relief," said Barbara. "But eventually she had to join her."

Catching her eye again, Roger laughed. "Behind the marble tomb there was also a cemetery for Irish wolfhounds. And one for rabbits."

They left without buying anything.

Sister Judith sat behind a desk. "A torpedo with a silver shell," thought Barbara apprehensively. Sister Judith's voice was deceptively small and carried Barbara instantly back to an atmosphere of disinfectant, grubby jackets, varnished wood, and chalk dust: Sister Kathleen was criticizing her penmanship. Barbara wondered if it was possible for people ever really to change.

"What a pity," Sister Judith said. "I'm very much afraid, Miss Dominick, that we can't help you. As you know, our budget is strictly limited."

"I have an idea." Barbara leaned forward and opened her portfolio.

Sister Judith listened, as motionless as the black crucifix on the wall behind her.

Barbara distributed thirty photographs, learning in the process that no dealer, from Roger Biscay to the tattooed hucksters at the swap meets, wanted to hear about stolen property. So she lied. She told an elaborate story about an interior decorator, a painter of still lifes, and a prop for an opera. Lewis listened to all this but did nothing himself. And still the rug was gone.

After the false telephone calls and letters were done, she turned to the nuns' new windows. Summer arrived: Barbara fell into her old habit of working in her studio late at night, when it was cooler, even though Lewis kept construction workers' hours. More and more, they ate and slept at different times and spoke infrequently. It was quiet, not like the thunderous misery of her first marriage, but one night when she slipped into bed after midnight Lewis sat bolt upright.

"You scared me," Barbara said.

Orange light inflated the bedroom, and she shaded her eyes.

"I haven't seen you since Monday," he said.

"I'm almost finished."

"With what?"

"The chapel." She drew up the sheet cautiously.

"Let's forget about the burglary and get a new rug," said Lewis.

"No."

"Why the hell not?"
"Stolen property sometimes turns up after a few months."
"I'm tired of this, Barb," Lewis said. "Tired of living with a spook, tired of keeping my things in a cardboard box. It's time to go on."
"So go! This is the way I am. I'm not a Barb."
He looked at her steadily. "Barb as in thorn. Barb as in wire."
"I warned you not to marry me."
Lewis lay back down, his arms behind his head, and stared at the cracked ceiling. The flesh of his face, like a fruit just past ripeness, showed areas of subtle decline. She felt a sharp pang of love; she wanted to make a picture of him. "Gray dulling everything. Our lives are half over," she thought.
"Oh, Lewis," she cried. "Before, nobody could rob me."
"So. You abstain?"
"I'm afraid."
Apparently talking to himself, he said: "I once heard of a medieval tower with a flagstone floor. The slabs stayed tight and flat for seven hundred years. And then one day a big stone popped up. Underneath it a clump of mushrooms had sprouted—the spores must have been dormant all the time."
They lay with their sweaty elbows touching. Many moths scuffled around the light.

When she answered the telephone the first time the line was dead. Then it rang again.
"Barbara?" said the half-remembered voice. "This is Roger Biscay."
"Yes?"
"Nothing about your rug. Sorry if I got your hopes up. But I do have some new ones to show you."
"Lewis isn't here."
"You—or he—could stop by anytime."
"I'm busy right now," Barbara said, with a flutter in her chest.
"Come soon," Roger said. "They may sell. Why not come by yourself?"
She loaded the last window in the back of her truck and went to the hospital. When the panel was installed beside the others she sat in the back pew and looked around the chapel. Quite a few sizable pieces of glass had survived the burglar's attack, and Barbara had salvaged all she could, setting the bits of broken glass in thin bands of copper foil instead of thicker, weaker, duller lead. The nuns had chosen conventional designs. These were still visible but in an exploded form, welded together by intricate copper lines.

A middle-aged woman entered the chapel, moved to the front, and buried her face in her hands. They sat together in the colored light. Barbara's eyes watered from the weeks of strain, for the copper foil technique was difficult. Her fingers were sore and stained, she was losing money on the job, but she knew that these windows were better than the first set: she thought they were the best stained glass that she had ever done. It was more than reconstruction; it was growth. Gradually her stiff neck relaxed, and her fingers felt better. After keeping him out of the studio for months, she wanted Lewis to see this job—if he were still interested. The older woman wept softly, and Barbara, suddenly ashamed, rose and left the hospital.

Her telephone rang while she wrestled with the new locks on the front door.

"Yes?" she said breathlessly.

"Did you lose a red Navajo rug?"

"Yes. What—"

"Would you pay a thousand-dollar reward?"

"Yes. Who is this?"

"I think I saw your rug at a swap meet."

"How—"

"I want to talk to your husband."

"You can talk to me."

The caller hung up.

"It was a man's voice," she told Lewis at the end of the afternoon. "A stranger, I think. How did he know I was married?"

"He may not call back," Lewis warned, but she could see his excitement. "I never thought this would happen."

The telephone rang.

During the second call the man told Lewis that the rug was two hundred miles away. By the third call, a few minutes later, some magic had brought the rug to Tucson, where it had been bought by innocent friends of the caller. If Lewis produced the money first, the caller would go get the rug. Lewis agreed to meet him early the next morning at a coffee shop.

"What are you doing now?" Barbara asked.

"Calling the cops, of course."

"They were all wearing jackets," Lewis said.

"In August?"

He looked shaken, Barbara thought.

"The coffee shop was full of guys in fatigue jackets with bulges at the shoulder. The police detective said just to introduce him as my friend Doug."

Barbara gripped his hand. "And the caller sat down anyway? What did he look like?"

"Just a little fellow," Lewis said. "Blow-dried. He didn't seem to mind Doug at all."

According to the go-between, the possessors of the rug were firm: they must be paid before they released the rug. Lewis had asked how he could be sure it was his rug.

"So he said, seriously, 'You have my word. I am a reputable textile dealer. I deal with Roger Biscay.' "

Then Doug had asked about the risks of dealing in stolen property.

"He didn't catch on?" said Barbara.

"No," said Lewis. "The little guy pointed to the empty chair at the table and he said, 'If a cop was sitting right there, I'd say the same thing.' I choked on my coffee."

"Then what?"

The detective had brought out his badge and asked the dealer to put his hands on the table. Instead, chairs and tables started turning over. The little man was running for the door. The police were shouting, "Freeze."

"Oh, I wish I'd been there," Barbara said.

"No, no. That would've been worse."

"What did you do?"

"Well," he said, embarrassed, "I knocked him into a plastic fern."

"Lewis!"

"He was pretty mad. He was shouting threats at me when they hauled him off. And then they made him take them to the rug."

They unfolded it upon the living room floor, stroking out the wrinkles and pulling the edges straight. The brilliant rectangle burned against the cement floor.

"Satisfied, Barb?"

She nodded. The wool made her bare knees and palms itch pleasurably as she studied it inch by inch.

"Look," she said. "A brown stain."

"Blood?"

"And look here."

In the midst of the border they saw a tiny charred spot.

"Maybe that was there before, hidden by the black dye," Lewis suggested.

Barbara knelt at one end. "I thought I knew this rug, but I was wrong. Come and see."

A red thread, nearly invisible, cut through the black border at the corner of the rug.

"A flaw?" she asked.

"No," said Lewis, kneeling too. "It's the spirit line, I guess. Every Navajo design is supposed to be imperfect, with an opening so the spirits won't be trapped. Sometimes it's called the weaver's pathway—on to another rug. A better one, maybe."

The telephone shrilled, and Barbara answered it.

"I'm a reputable textile dealer, and I earned my reward. You lied to me. Your husband assaulted me."

"Listen—" she began, but he had already hung up.

"I haven't been in a fight since the sixth grade." Lewis passed a hand over his face as though to discover whether the same features were there. "I didn't mean to hurt him."

In a moment the telephone rang again. This time there was no one at the other end, and Lewis and Barbara stared at each other.

"I feel sorry for him," Lewis said.

"It is our rug."

"Yes."

"Lewis," she said, "do you think Roger Biscay had anything to do with this? He called me this morning. But I thought he was just making a pass."

"He probably was making a pass," said Lewis evenly.

The ringing began again; they ignored it.

"We touched something bad," he said, troubled.

Barbara looked at the big red rug and tried to imagine the places where it had been, the hands that had touched it. "Oh, the lives of things," she thought suddenly.

"We'll never know," she said aloud.

The telephone stopped ringing.

"Is it safe to keep the rug here?" Lewis asked.

Barbara turned away. Flooded with sun, the little house now struck her as meager and vulnerable—hot in summer, cold in winter. She saw that the wicker furniture was worn out, the plaster cracked, the amount of space Spartan. She pictured a new stained glass window in a large and beautiful room with a Navajo rug on the floor. "Forest green," she thought. "Mahogany. Gold." She saw parties going on, with food being eaten and children at play. For the moment it all seemed possible. She put her arms around Lewis's neck and felt a pulse beating behind his ear.

"We'll move," she said.

Susan Lowell was born in Chihuahua City, Chihuahua, Mexico, in 1950 and has lived on both sides of the border. She is a fourth-generation Arizonan descended from ranchers, gold miners, explorers, artists, and schoolteachers. One of her grandfathers was a New Englander with a distant connection to the Lowells of Boston.

She has also lived in Italy, California, Utah, New Jersey, and Texas, graduating first from Stanford and then from Princeton. Arizona has always been home. She has worked as a newspaper reporter, a college teacher, and most recently as a fiction writer while raising two children.

Lowell and her husband Ross Humphreys have a small cattle ranch on the edge of the Tohono O'odham Reservation, at the base of Baboquivari Peak, which the Tohono O'odham Indians believe to be the center of the universe, sixteen miles north of Mexico.